SHAME

ON

ME

FOOL ME ONCE #2

Also by Tara Sivec

Fool Me Once Series

Shame On You

Chocolate Lovers Series

Seduction and Snacks
Futures and Frosting
Troubles and Treats
Hearts and Llamas
Chocolate Lovers Special Edition
Love and Lists

Playing with Fire Series

A Beautiful Lie
Because of You
Worn Me Down

Watch Over Me

Tara Sivec

SHAME

ON

ME

FOOL ME ONCE #2

Published by Montlake Romance, Seattle

www.apub.com

Amazon, the Amazon logo, and Montlake Romance are trademarks of Amazon.com, Inc., or its affiliates.

ISBN-13: 9781477801116
ISBN-10: 1477801111

Cover design by Erin Fitzsimmons

Library of Congress Control Number: 2013921707

Printed in the United States of America

For James—the only person I know with a bigger shoe addiction than Paige. I love you, even if you have better kicks than I do.

CHAPTER 1

D o I look okay? Am I showing enough cleavage?"

Lorelei stares me up and down, and in an uncharacteristic move from my slightly uptight best friend, she reaches out and unbuttons the top button of the already-plunging neck of my halter vest. I was almost popping out of my top as it was. Now I'm going to have to hold my breath to keep the girls contained.

"There, that's better. Let's go."

As we walk side by side into Sean O'Casey's Irish Pub, I put on my game face. Tonight, I'm not Paige McCarty, world-renowned model; I am Paige McCarty—man bait. My best friends Lorelei Warner and Kennedy O'Brien and I own our own private investigative firm called Fool Me Once Investigations, which was started after we were all screwed over by the men in our lives.

My ex—he threw away our entire life savings on his gambling habit. Do you want to know how I found out that Andy had a gambling problem? I had just found a pair of Christian Louboutins that were TO DIE for. Seriously. Black slingbacks with a peep toe, silver spike embellishments, and a black bow with spikes right by the toe. I almost cried. Actually, I did cry when all three of my credit cards were declined when I took the shoes up to the counter to pay for them. Maxed out. Over the limit. No more shoe purchases that day, or maybe ever. I figured it was just some sort of mistake until the snotty store clerk handed over the phone when she called the credit card company. Six hundred thousand dollars' worth of debt. I know I have a slight problem when it comes to buying shoes, but not a six-hundred-thousand-dollar problem!

I confronted Andy that night when he got home from work, and the weasel broke down sobbing in the middle of our living room. He racked up that much debt in just three short months. Three months of flying to Vegas and Atlantic City when he was supposed to be in Silicon Valley at software conferences.

Lying sack of shit.

But right now, I don't have time to think about how much I still want to strangle my ex, because I have a job to do. I have a cheating husband to catch in the act. A man by the name of Matt Russo.

⬤

"All right, so according to his file, Matt is a graphic designer and his wife, Melanie, says he's been spending too much time away from the house and not enough time with her." Lorelei fills me in as we walk through O'Casey's.

Lorelei has been doing some light surveillance of him the past few weeks: staking out his place, following him to work—that sort of thing. Since his wife swears she's seen texts from another woman on his phone, and he's been extra secretive around her lately, it's time to up our game. Lorelei never saw him doing anything suspicious like sneaking out at lunch with his arm around a bimbo.

And this is where I come in: the bimbo.

"I already hate the bastard and I haven't even met him. Why do men feel the need to lie? If you're not happy, just tell us. We'll help you pack," I complain.

My heels click on the floor of the pub as I make my way over to the bar. Tonight I'm wearing one of my favorite bait outfits: a nice little ensemble I like to call "my eyes are up here, moron." My top is a gray pinstripe halter vest: completely backless and held together in the front with just four tiny buttons. Well, three buttons now, thanks to Lorelei. If I make sure not to take deep breaths, my all-natural 34Cs should stay put.

"I see him—over there at the end of the bar, nursing a beer," Lorelei says quietly next to me.

My gaze zeroes in on our subject and I take a moment to watch him unnoticed. He looks exactly like his picture in the file. Black hair, short on the sides and messy on top; dark stubble around a jaw that I can't deny is a little delicious to look at; and a pair of black, trendy glasses perched on his nose. My ex wore a pair of those glasses. He didn't need glasses, but he thought they made him look cool.

They didn't.

Matt is wearing a blue-and-white-striped button-down with a navy blue V-necked sweater over it with a pair of khaki dress pants. Nerdy chic. Super. It's like someone packaged up Andy and stuck him in this bar just for me. Remind me again why I picked this job instead of the easy subpoena delivery that Lorelei got?

"Wow, he looks a lot like Andy," Lorelei says, stating the obvious.

"I know. Don't remind me. I kind of want to slam his face into the bar right now."

Lorelei pulls a small Nikon camera out of her purse and checks the zoom lens.

"Please refrain from beating up the subject until I can get a good shot of him making out with you," she tells me in a bored voice before putting the camera back in her bag.

Right. The job. Fool Me Once Investigations was started because the three of us wanted to help other women avoid looking like fools when the men in their lives played them. We take other cases to help pay the bills, but coming to the rescue of our fellow woman scorned is what we prefer. I need to remember that this is just a job and not a way for me to channel my anger at Andy through someone else. All I have to do is make nice with the little cheater, chat him up, buy him a few drinks, and then get him to kiss me. Piece of cake and bam, the wife is vindicated and can happily take her photos to her lawyer. I've done it a hundred times.

Oh, don't look at me like that—I'm not a whore. Even though my mother seems to think I am whenever I tell her I'm out on another job. They say you have to kiss a few frogs before you meet your Prince Charming. Well, I'm kissing a thousand frogs to show other women that Prince Charming will screw you over the first chance he gets.

"Okay, wish me luck," I tell Lorelei before fluffing my hair and strutting over to the bar. Just like always, Lorelei takes a seat at one of the booths across from the bar with a clear view of the subject. We've done this so many times together that we've got it down to a science. All I have to do is say my name and no matter who the guy is, his eyes will light up with recognition. I know, that makes me sound a little conceited, but I swear I'm not. It's the truth.

I used to like the fact that whenever I told a guy my name you could see his mind racing as he remembered all of the pictures he'd seen of me on magazine covers. It made me feel special and wanted and beautiful. Now it's just annoying. Just once it would be nice for a guy to have no idea who I am—to like me for me. To be with a guy who has no expectation that you will look magazine-cover ready first thing in the morning.

Andy liked having arm candy for a wife. He liked taking me out and showing me off. It was sweet at first, and then it got old. He wasn't happy just sitting at home on a Friday night, wearing sweats and watching a movie. He always wanted to show me off to his friends.

Fucking Andy!

Sliding onto the bar stool next to Matt, I signal the waiter and he comes rushing over.

"I'll take a lemon-drop martini and one of whatever this handsome man next to me is having," I tell the bartender with a wink.

Matt looks up from his drink and blinks at me in surprise.

Wow, he has really blue eyes. Like, really blue. And he smells delicious. That cologne is making my girly bits tingle. I'm pretty sure it's Burberry Touch. I have a nose for good cologne.

"Oh, thanks, but I'm good," he tells me with a distracted smile before looking back down at his half-empty glass of beer.

Um, okaaaay. Let's try this again.

"Hi, I'm Paige," I tell him brightly, sticking my hand out in front of him.

"Oh, hi. Matthew," he tells me distractedly.

His warm hand engulfs mine and he shakes it once before pulling it away and going right back to looking down in his glass.

Fine. On to Plan B.

"It's Paige McCarty, by the way," I tell him sweetly, enunciating my last name. I was on the cover of *Maxim* last month. He'll be asking for an autographed copy in three seconds.

"Did you say McCarty?" he asks, finally looking up and staring at my face.

Here we go . . .

"I sure did, handsome," I tell him with a wink.

God, this is nauseating. I really am better than this. I need to talk to Kennedy about putting me on some different jobs. This is getting to be too degrading.

"My mother is Irish. Her maiden name was McCarty."

I do nothing but sit here staring at him with my mouth open. He could be lying, considering he's a cheater and that's what they're good at, but something tells me he seriously has no idea who I am. My spidey senses are not screaming "lying sack of shit" right at this moment. Obviously, they're on the fritz. A woman doesn't just fork over a couple of grand to have her husband investigated for cheating. She has suspicions and it's my job to make sure they are validated, not question the authenticity of this guy's morals.

Matt slides off of his stool and throws a twenty down on top of the bar.

"Well, it was nice meeting you, Paige McCarty. Be careful on your way home. This isn't the best neighborhood for a woman to be alone in at night."

And with that, Matt gives me a polite nod, turns, and walks out of the bar—without even attempting to flirt with me or ask me to go home with him.

Shame on me for thinking this job was going to be a piece of cake.

CHAPTER 2

"I'm thinking of wearing jeans and a nice tank top to dinner with Griffin tonight. What do you think?"

I look up at Kennedy as she paces back and forth in front of my desk. Kennedy is going on her first official date with Griffin tonight. They've been hot and heavy for a few weeks working on a bail-jumper case and due to some genius thinking on Griffin's part, he finally got Kennedy to go on a real date with him. I'm pretty sure it's going to be the highlight of her family's week, since they've wanted the two of them together forever.

"You cannot dress like a hobo to go on a date with Griffin." I shake my head at her and she rolls her eyes at me.

"Jeans and a tank are not hobo wear."

"Kennedy, comfort should not be your first order of business when planning your attire for the evening. It should be picking an outfit that makes him want to skip the date just to rip your clothes off."

Kennedy sits down at her desk in a huff and crosses her arms in front of her.

"This is dumb. We already skipped to that part. Several times. I don't know why this date is such a big deal."

"It's a big deal because it's romantic and sweet. Griffin wants to treat you well and prove to you that he's not with you just for sex. Wear something red and show off your legs," I tell her, powering up my laptop.

"Please tell me you're not suggesting I wear a dress," she grumbles.

"You're wearing a dress. You're also going to wear heels. Quit your bitching."

While Kennedy moans and groans about stupid men and something about seeing her in a dress at prom if he wouldn't have ditched her, I decide against asking her how to find more information on Matt Russo. She's got enough on her plate tonight. Going right to Google, I type in Matt's name and wait for the hits to load.

"I'm guessing I can't just stop at Walmart on my way home and find this red dress you speak of, can I?" Kennedy asks as she grabs her keys from her desk and stands up.

"If you buy a dress from Walmart for this date, I will disown you."

Turning away from my computer, I dig into my purse, pull out a business card, and hand it to her. "Go to Nordstrom and ask for Alicia. She used to be my personal shopper, you know, before Andy decided all my hard-earned money should be flushed down the toilet. She will find you something amazing."

Kennedy looks at the card for a few seconds and then shoves it into the back pocket of her jeans as her dad, Buddy, walks through the front door of the office. "I feel like Julia Roberts in *Pretty Woman*. Except I'm not a hooker."

"Can you please tell that to my friends at the VFW? They're still asking me about the escort service ad Griffin ran in the newspaper last week. They're concerned that you aren't returning their calls because you used the Google on them and saw that they're all old as dirt," Buddy states. "I reassured them that you are a good person and would never discriminate based on age."

During Kennedy and Griffin's brief courtship, if that's what you want to call it, Griffin decided to get back at Kennedy for a joke we played on him by placing an ad in the local paper that said Fool Me Once Investigations was an escort service. Buddy is having a hard time coming to terms with the fact that it's not true.

"Dad, still not a hooker. How about you just tell them that?"

Buddy looks at her like she's insane. "I'm the most popular guy at the VFW right now, Kennedy. People yell my name when I walk in and everyone buys me drinks. I'm not about to kill my popularity. This is the only thing I have to live for. Don't deny me this."

Kennedy gives up the argument for today, kisses Buddy on the cheek, and heads out of the office, hopefully to buy a dress.

"Okay, now that she's gone, here's the plan for tonight. The whole family is going to stop by so we can see Kennedy and Griffin off on their date," Buddy whispers to me, looking over his shoulder to make sure Kennedy didn't sneak back in.

"You know she's going to kill you, right? She doesn't want to make a big deal out of this."

Buddy shrugs and backs toward the door. "My daughter is finally dating Griffin. I never thought I'd see the day those two would finally get their heads out of their asses. I want a front-row seat so I can make sure it actually happens and she doesn't chicken out."

I laugh at Buddy and he gives me a small wave over his shoulder before walking out the door.

Once he's gone, I get back to my Google search. The file we have on Matt isn't very detailed, since all we really need to know about Matt for this case is where he'll be at certain times of the day so we can follow him. He's not a criminal—that we know of—so Lorelei didn't need to do an extensive court-record search on him. And he didn't break the law, so Kennedy doesn't need to hunt him down and kick his ass.

I know my job is to just sit and look pretty, but I'm tired of that nonsense. I'm smart and resourceful; maybe if I go above and beyond my typical duties, Kennedy will trust me to handle some real cases. Cases where I need to learn to shoot a gun and put my newly learned self-defense moves to work.

Sure, looking deeper into Matt Russo's background isn't going to have me running through the streets chasing down bad guys, but at least it will show that I'm taking initiative.

"Well, hello, twenty-five Matt Russo Facebook pages. Let's see, only one is from South Bend, so let's go with that," I say aloud, clicking on his name.

"Wonderful. Profile is set to private. What the hell, Matt? No one sets their profile to private unless they have something to hide. Do you have something to hide, Mr. Russo?"

Backing out of Facebook, I click on the next site that Google found on him: LinkedIn.

Let's see here. Matt Russo is a graphic designer currently employed by Bolder Design Studio. I already knew this information, so this isn't helping me at all. He's an art nerd just like my ex is a computer nerd. No matter how cute he was last night, he's probably just as much of a tool as Andy. I don't know why that thought makes me sad. I don't even know the guy. Just because he didn't recognize me in the bar last night doesn't mean he's a stand-up person without a secret girlfriend.

But man alive, those blue eyes . . . I wonder what they would look like without the glasses. I wonder if they would darken if he was in my bed and I was taking his pants off.

Shit! What the hell is wrong with me? Matt Russo will not be in my bed, ever.

There's a reason why I'm always attracted to nerdy assholes. I don't know what that reason is right now, but I'm sure there is one. I am going to focus on finding out if Matt Russo is really a cheater and that's it. I am not going to think about whether or not he's got a six-pack hiding under that sweater vest.

Deciding to nip this thing in the bud, I pick up my phone and dial the receptionist at Bolder Design Studio. The sooner I can end this case, the sooner I can find a hot guy who looks and acts nothing like my ex and bang the memory of glasses-wearing, sweater-vest-donning, computer geeks out of my system.

While the phone rings, I clear my throat and put on my best dumb-blonde act.

"Bolder Design, how can I help you?" the receptionist answers.

"Hi, this is Chloe-with-an-e Marin," I respond with a giggle, using the name of the woman Kennedy found her husband boning when she came home from a tour in Afghanistan. "You're going to think I am such an idiot, but I was supposed to have a meeting with Mr. Russo this evening so he could help me design my new adult video website and I TOTALLY forgot the time and where we're supposed to meet."

I know I'm laying it on thick. *Whatever.* I hate that Chloe bitch and I firmly believe she does porn on the side.

"Hold on just one second. Let me pull up Mr. Russo's calendar."

I giggle again for added effect while I hear her clicking away at her computer through the line.

"Here we go. Hmmm, I don't see anything on his calendar with you tonight, Miss Marin. He does have a dinner scheduled at Blake's Seafood at five, but he must have forgotten to add your name."

I'd like to thank the Academy . . .

"That's it! Blake's at five. You are such a doll!"

I quickly thank the clueless woman and disconnect the call. Glancing at the clock on the wall, I see that I have an hour and a half before I need to get to Blake's. Just enough time to run home and freshen up. I'm assuming that Matt is smart enough not to put the name of his rendezvous location with his suspected mistress on his work calendar, but you never know. Running over to Lorelei's desk, I grab the Nikon out of the top drawer and shove it into my purse. Maybe I'll get lucky and catch him canoodling with a waitress in a dark corner. I can snap a picture and be gone, never to think of naked Matt Russo again.

CHAPTER 3

Walking through the door of Blake's Seafood Restaurant, I scan my reflection in the mirror next to the hostess station. I know it doesn't matter what I'm wearing since I plan on hiding in a corner and spying on Matt, but it's impossible for me to go out in public without looking good. Every once in a while I'm recognized by a fan, which is actually a plus in this line of work, because the guy I'm trying to catch cheating would never suspect that I'm an investigator.

I kept it casual tonight with a royal blue cotton strapless dress that falls right above my knees with a matching pair of blue open-toed Gucci heels. Signaling to the hostess on the phone that I was just going to head to the bar, I make my way into the main part of the restaurant and to the corner of the bar closest to me. With my back to the wall and a drink menu up in front of my face, I peer over the top, scoping out the restaurant. I immediately spy Matt on the other side of the room in his own dark corner.

Mmm-hmmm, just what I thought. Hiding in a corner—all the better to make out with your mistress. Ordering a glass of white wine, I crouch low on my stool and keep an eye on Mr. Cheater McCheatpants.

After an hour, two more glasses of wine, and seven shredded cocktail napkins, my ass is starting to fall asleep on the bar stool and I actually catch myself yawning. This is pathetic. What kind of a cheater is this guy? All he's done in the last sixty minutes is look at the screen on his cell phone and glance toward the door over and over again. Maybe his home-wrecker girlfriend stood him up. Serves the guy right.

Sliding off of the bar stool, I work out the kinks in my legs from sitting so long, staying close to the shadows in the corner. Turning back around quickly to make sure I don't miss anything from Matt's table, I slam right into a solid chest and my hands immediately press against it to steady myself. The smell of Burberry Touch cologne tingles my nose and butterflies flap rapidly in my stomach as I lift my head.

"Hey, you're the woman from last night. Paige, right?"

Oh, shit. I've been made. Kennedy is going to kill me.

I stare into Matt's eyes as he smiles down at me, his hands still holding tightly to my arms. It could be the wine talking right now, but Jesus, he's really good-looking up close. He's removed his glasses and his sparkling blue eyes are staring right down at my face, taking in everything he sees.

"What are the odds that we'd run into each other again?" Matt asks, the dimple in his left cheek forming when he cocks one side of his mouth up in a grin.

Oh, pretty good, considering I'm following you.

"It's definitely a nice coincidence," I tell him with a sultry smile. I don't care if he smells like heaven and I have a weakness for dimples, I'm still here to do a job. Since I can no longer lurk in a dark corner and spy on him, maybe I can ply him with alcohol and get him to talk. It didn't work last night, but he doesn't seem as preoccupied as he did then. "Are you here alone?"

Matt nods his head and lets out a sigh. "I am. Is it pathetic that I'm sitting in the corner of a bar by myself on a Friday night?"

He laughs easily at himself and runs a hand through his hair, making the spikes messy, and for some reason I want to reach up and smooth them back down.

"Well, it looks like we're both pretty pathetic tonight, since I was doing the same thing," I tell him as I gesture over to my pile of shredded napkins on the bar next to my empty wineglasses.

"Several glasses of wine AND mutilated napkins. You must be having a bad week," he laughs.

"One of my best friends fell madly in love and I have to go to a party later on tonight to toast to their happiness. Let's just say it's a good thing the bartender didn't put any knives in front of me tonight."

Matt chuckles and shakes his head. "Those napkins never stood a chance. At least now I know to keep sharp objects far out of your reach."

A laugh bubbles up out of me before I can catch it. "I'm happy for them. Really, I am. I only think about stabbing my ex in the heart four times a day now instead of seven."

"See? That's progress right there. Pretty soon you'll only be thinking about lighting all of his things on fire," Matt replies with a chuckle.

"Oh, that ship has already sailed. You always burn their shit first, then you daydream about chopping off body parts."

"I feel like this conversation escalated very quickly," Matt says with another laugh and a raise of one eyebrow.

I have no idea why I even told him about Kennedy or Andy; it just spilled out of me. I've never spoken to subjects about anything other than how good they look and how much money they make. In this line of work, it's always about them. Do whatever you can to make them feel special and important and they'll be eating out of your hands in no time. It's never taken me more than a few minutes to get a guy to show his true colors. A couple of seconds alone with Matt and I'm laughing and forgetting why I'm here.

Taking a deep breath, I slide my hands off of his chest and take a few steps back. I need to get into character.

"Would you like to have a drink with me?" I ask, gesturing to the bar stool next to mine.

Matt looks back at the door for a moment. My hackles immediately go up when I realize he's probably trying to decide if he should keep waiting for his "date" or take a chance on scoring with a new girl. He's probably calculating the odds in his head and part of me hopes he'll turn me down. What kind of a man cheats on his wife and cheats on his mistress? That's just gross. When he turns back to face me with a smile and a shrug, I want to kick my own ass for being attracted to this douchebag.

"Sure, I'll take you up on that drink. I think I owe you one anyway. I was kind of a dick last night," he explains as he pulls out my stool for me and waits for me to sit down before taking his own seat.

"It's fine. We all have bad nights," I tell him with a reassuring smile as I lean my elbows on the bar so I'm closer to him.

"You can say that again. Although right now, I think I'm having more of a bad life instead of a bad week."

Geez, this guy is really that depressed that his mistress stood him up? His poor wife. Why the hell didn't I think of bringing a recorder with me? It would be a lot easier to just tape all this shit he's spewing than try to get him to make out with me. Shit! The camera is in my purse. Now that I'm not going to be able to catch him with his mistress, I'm back to Plan A and need to get him to kiss me.

"Would you excuse me for a minute? I need to go to the ladies' room."

I give him a wink, grab my purse from the bar, and quickly head toward the hostess station, glancing back over my shoulder to make sure he's not watching me.

Pulling the camera and a hundred-dollar bill out of my purse, I set the items down right in front of the hostess.

"I need you to do me a huge favor. I'll give you another hundred dollars if you can get a few good pictures of me making out with that guy I'm sitting next to at the bar," I tell her quickly, pointing to Matt, who still has his back to us and is chatting with the bartender.

"Awww, how sweet! Why don't I just come over there now and take a picture? You don't have to pay me," the young girl replies happily.

"No, no, no. He can't know the picture is being taken. I'm a private investigator."

She looks at me in awe for a few minutes as I check over my shoulder again to make sure Matt is preoccupied.

"Wow. Are you, like, undercover? Do you work for the government? Am I being taped right now?" she whispers.

Rolling my eyes, I back away from the hostess stand.

"Yeah, sure. It's top-secret government work. I could tell you about it, but then I'd have to kill you," I reply with seriousness.

Don't judge me. I'll do whatever it takes right now.

"You can count on me." She salutes me and clutches the camera close to her chest.

With a sigh, I turn around and rush back to Matt's side.

"I ordered you another glass of white wine; I hope that's okay," he tells me with a smile as I take my seat next to him.

"Perfect, thank you." I reach up and place my hand on his bicep, giving it a gentle squeeze, and act like it's perfectly natural for me to be touching him—all part of the job. If you're touchy-feely with a subject, it will make them more inclined to be touchy-feely with you.

Rubbing my palm up and down his arm, I swallow thickly. Holy hell, he's got some muscles hidden under that button-down. I have to forcibly remove my hand from his arm, otherwise I might start looking for more muscle. Needing something to do with my hand other than molest him, I pick up my glass of wine and take a healthy swallow.

"So, what do you do for a living, Paige McCarty?"

The wine immediately goes down the wrong pipe and I begin coughing and sputtering. Matt reaches up and gently pats me on the back as I set my wineglass down. When I'm finally able to catch my breath, I turn to look into his eyes to see if he's serious. I still find it hard to believe he has no idea who I am. There isn't a man alive under the age of fifty who doesn't know who I am. Maybe this is part of his shtick; his way of trying to charm me. Fine, Mr. Russo. We'll play it your way.

"Actually, I'm a model," I reply with a smile.

He blinks in surprise and if I didn't know any better, I'd say it was genuine. "Wow, no kidding? Have you done a lot of work or are you just starting out?"

It's my turn to stare at him in shock. This guy is really good. I almost believe him. I'm going to need to stay at the top of my game with him.

"Oh, just a few jobs here and there. Nothing you would have seen."

Why the hell am I lying to him? What difference does it make if he knows how famous I am?

"Good for you. I hope someday I can see you in something, but the only magazines I read are ones about graphic design," he says with a shrug.

"I wish my ex only read graphic design magazines. He subscribed to more magazines than any woman I've ever met so he could pimp me out to every magazine editor he could find."

Shut up, Paige. He doesn't need to know your life story!

"All my ex cared about was my money, so it looks like we both made huge mistakes in our lives," Matt confides.

Wait, ex? Is he talking about Melanie or another ex? According to what Melanie told Kennedy, they're still married.

"So you're divorced?"

Matt sighs deeply and takes a sip of his Jack and Coke. "Separated. Honestly, we probably should have never even gotten married. We met in college and all of my friends tried to warn me about her. She didn't show her true colors to me until we were married, though."

And now the investigator in me wants to know everything about her. Purely for business purposes, of course. It has nothing to do with the fact that he's easy on the eyes.

"What kind of true colors are we talking here? Crazy possessive female or was she really a man?" I ask, trying to get him to smile again.

It does the trick. He barks out a laugh. "No, definitely not a man. I'm pretty sure she only married me because she saw the dollar signs. She's going to try and take my father's company and there's no way I can let that happen."

I take a sip of my wine so I'm not tempted to reach out and comfort him. "Wow, that's not good. I'm so sorry."

Matt shrugs. "And to add more to my pathetic life story, I'm positive she's been cheating on me. All I need is proof so I can end this bullshit charade of hers and make sure the company stays in the family."

My mouth drops open at all he's admitted to me. He could be lying. This could be how he gets chicks—by laying it on thick and playing the "woe is me" card, but something tells me that's not the case. His voice immediately takes on a tone of sadness when he talks about his father's company, and my senses are screaming at me that he's telling the truth.

"You think your wife is cheating on you?" I whisper.

This is too weird. Even for me.

"I can't believe I'm telling you this. I barely know you and I feel like a jackass for unloading all of this on you right now. You're a really easy person to talk to."

He feels like a jackass? I feel like a jackass. I should just tell him right now that his wife hired me to find out if he is cheating, but I can't. I can't do anything until I know for sure.

"We haven't been happy for a really long time. Fuck. We were probably never really happy. A friend of mine told me she was going to be here and I guess I was just hoping to finally have a solid reason for not wanting to be married to her," he admits.

Jesus, the two of us could be a match made in heaven under different circumstances. Finding out Andy had a gambling problem had been just the catalyst I needed to kick his ass to the curb.

"What are you going to do if you find out it's true and she's really cheating on you?" I ask.

"If I have proof that she's been unfaithful, I can threaten to out her to her family as a cheater. She'll leave the company alone so they never know her perfect character is tarnished."

Goddammit all to hell! I believe him. I believe him and now I want to help him. This is not good.

"I'm sorry. I wish there was something I could do."

Tell him the truth! Tell him his wife hired you and you feel awful and want to help him instead.

Before I can open my mouth and make a huge mistake, I watch as Matt's eyes widen as he stares across the bar.

"Oh, shit. She's here," Matt says under his breath, ducking his head to hide behind me.

Turning my head, I see his wife, Melanie, coming through the doorway on the arm of a very large, very badass-looking man who's got to be twice her age.

"She's heading this way. Matt, she's totally going to see you. Shit! Hide under the bar!"

Matt tries turning sideways to quickly dive under the bar, but his elbow slams into my glass, knocking it over and spilling wine down the front of my dress.

I let out a squeal as the cold liquid seeps through my dress and Matt quickly grabs a pile of napkins and starts blotting at my boobs. My breath gets caught in my throat as he presses his hands against my breasts and glances over his shoulder distractedly to see where Melanie is. He turns back and notices the shocked expression on my face and his eyes drop to his hand that is now just resting casually on my boob, practically cupping it.

I tear my eyes away from his hand and how good it feels against my chest and see that Melanie and her beefcake are a few feet away at this point and heading right toward us. If she looks away from her date, she's going to look right at Matt. There's not even any time for him to get up and run to the bathroom. He'll barrel right into her. Suddenly, the tables have turned and I'm on Matt's side. I want him to catch her in the act. I want him to be vindicated so he can move on with his life.

"Do something!"

Before all of the words finish leaving my mouth, I feel Matt's arms wrap around my waist and I'm hauled out of my stool and pulled between his legs. His mouth is on mine immediately and I don't even think about what I'm doing. I wrap my arms around his neck and pull him closer.

CHAPTER 4

I hear the click of Melanie's heels as she walks past us and I know by now that we're in the clear and can pull away, but I stopped caring about anything as soon as I felt Matt's lips against mine. And when his tongue touches mine, I forget all about the fact that we're in a crowded restaurant making out. His lips are firm and his tongue is soft and this kiss is the best thing I've experienced in my entire life.

As he softly explores my mouth, I pull him closer and mold my body against his. I'm suddenly wishing we were anywhere but here. Somewhere I could straddle his hips and feel him between my legs. The kiss goes on and on as I tangle my fingers in his hair and hold him close, moaning softly into his mouth when he switches angles and deepens the kiss. I feel like I can't get enough of him and by the way his arms band tightly around me and hold me close, I know he feels the same.

The only thing that interrupts us is the soft sound of someone clearing her throat behind me.

"Sorry to bother you. Just checking to see if you guys need a refill or if there's anything I can do for you."

Regretfully ending the kiss, I turn my head without letting go of Matt and see the hostess standing next to us. She quite obviously winks at me and I realize that my fingers are still threaded through Matt's hair and his hands are dangerously close to my ass.

And I'm guessing by the sneaky look on this girl's face that she just got a bunch of awesome pictures of the two of us with my camera.

"Nope, we're good, thanks." I try to tell her with my eyes that she should go away but she doesn't get the hint.

"Really, I'm here to help. Would you like me to do anything else for you?" she stresses. She attempts to wink at me again, her way of letting me know she got the photos. The way her face contorts makes it look like she's having a stroke.

"Miss, are you okay?" Matt asks her in concern, his arms still holding me close.

"Oh! Ha, ha, I'm great! I just wanted to let you know that if I can be of service, I'm here."

She stands there staring at us, not making any move to walk away.

"Wow, they're really accommodating to their customers," Matt whispers in my ear. His warm breath gives me goose bumps and I realize I have completely lost control of this situation. Sure, I was starting to believe him, and seeing his wife show up on the arm of another man solidified the story he told me, but being this distracted by a simple kiss is not like me at all. I have no idea what I'm supposed to do now.

Under normal circumstances, I'd be feeling pretty smug that I was able to get the money shot of a subject, but I just feel dirty. I feel awful that I didn't come clean with Matt when he poured his heart out to me. Now all I can think about is that kiss and when we can do it again.

I am so going to get fired.

"Okay. Well, I'll just be over there, by the hostess stand, if you need anything," she states with another awkward wink in my direction. As she turns and walks away, I can see a bulge in her front pocket that I know is my camera. My camera filled with shots of me kissing Matt. Shots that I want to look at over and over again alone at home.

When the girl is finally gone, I turn my face back to Matt. He's staring at my lips and I can't stop my tongue from sliding out and running over them, savoring the taste of him still there. Matt suddenly lets go of me when he realizes his arms are still wrapped tightly around me long after the threat of being spotted by his ex is gone. I immediately miss the warmth of his body.

"I feel like I should apologize for using you like that," he tells me as I take a step back from him, his eyes still focused on my lips.

"And I feel like I should tell you that there's no apology necessary, and you can feel free to use me like that anytime."

We both laugh a little uncomfortably. Matt cranes his neck, searching around the restaurant. "I don't see Melanie anywhere. They must have been seated in another room."

Heat flushes through me when I remember the whole reason for the kiss: to make sure his estranged wife didn't see him. I feel like I've waited my entire life for a kiss like that. And now I have to get up from this bar stool and walk away from him and never see him again. It would be unethical for me to do anything else. He's not cheating on his wife, so this case is closed. I can't help him any more than I already have. I've already compromised Fool Me Once Investigations enough for one night.

❧

Kennedy's family, along with Lorelei, Griffin, and me, are all standing around our offices waiting for Kennedy to finally come out of the bathroom. Earlier, I was happy to come here tonight and toast my best friend and her newfound love. Now, I'm preoccupied and freaked out that someone is going to ask me about the case.

It's been an hour since I left Matt at the bar. Actually, it's been one hour, eight minutes, and thirty-five seconds. But who's counting?

Me! I'm counting!

I can still feel his lips on mine, and I can still hear the anguish in his voice when he told me about his wife cheating on him and trying to take away his father's company. He's a good man; I can feel it. I want to beat that bitch Melanie to the ground, but I can't. She signed a contract with us and we have clearly defined rules and regulations in that contract that state there will be no conflict of interest and that everything we do will be to protect our client. Matt isn't our client, Melanie is. Melanie: the gold-digging whore.

I listen distractedly as everyone talks around me, wondering if Kennedy would let me quit for a week so I don't violate the contract by helping Matt.

"Oh, speaking of whores, what's going on with that case of yours, Paige? Weren't you working on catching some slutty guy whose wife suspected him of cheating?"

The swallow I take of champagne goes down the wrong pipe immediately when Kennedy's brother, Ted, questions me. I cough and try to take a breath as he comes over and pats me on the back, adding more champagne to my glass.

I feel my cheeks redden, and I look away from Ted quickly, chugging the entire glass of champagne in one swallow.

"Guy? What guy? There's no guy. I don't know a guy. Who wants more champagne?" I ask, grabbing the bottle from Ted's hand and walking away.

Thank God Kennedy walks in the room at that moment and I don't have to acknowledge the questioning look he's shooting at me.

Standing by the wall on the opposite side of the room, I forgo my champagne glass and drink directly out of the bottle while everyone fawns over Kennedy in her short red dress and awesome Jimmy Choo shoes that I let her borrow. No one cares that I'm drowning my sorrows in cheap champagne.

"Did you just drink directly out of that bottle? What's going on with you?"

I sigh and rest my head against the wall as Lorelei folds her arms and raises her eyebrows at me, waiting for me to talk.

"Nothing is wrong. This champagne is just delicious. I didn't feel like waiting to pour it into my glass. It's such a waste of time."

"Nice try. Give me the bottle," Lorelei demands, holding her hand out to me.

I reluctantly hand it to her and glance over her shoulder at Kennedy and Griffin, wrapped up in each other's arms, staring into each other's eyes.

I want that for myself. I didn't think I did, but I really do. I miss having someone look at me like that. Like I'm his whole world. I don't really know Matt. I certainly don't trust him; I doubt I'll ever really trust another man again. But I can't deny that kissing him made me remember what it was like to have someone special in my life. I want more than an empty condo to go home to and a job where I have to be a liar and kind of slutty. I want to stand for something. I want what I do to mean something, and I feel like helping Matt is just the ticket I need to show people that I have a brain.

"Were you able to track down Matt Russo again?" Lorelei questions, bringing me out of my depressing thoughts.

"Ummm, yep. I tracked him down."

Lorelei stares at me, waiting for me to elaborate.

"Doesn't Kennedy look great in that dress? I'm so happy for her and Griffin," I muse.

Lorelei narrows her eyes at me and when I bite my lip and try to reach for the champagne bottle, her eyes widen.

"Paige, what did you do?" she demands.

"Give me the champagne."

She holds it farther from my reach and I cross my arms in front of me, refusing to let her force me to tell her what happened. This is my problem and I'm going to deal with it.

"Tell me you didn't. Paige, did you compromise the case? Did you tell him what you were hired to do?"

I immediately get defensive. I'm not an idiot. I'm just confused. "No! I didn't tell him what I was there for!"

At least I'm not lying about that part.

"Okay, so what's the problem then? Were you unable to get any good photos of him cheating? It's no big deal if it takes you a few tries," Lorelei says.

"There's no problem. I got the photos and everything is fine," I tell her with a sigh.

Lorelei turns and we see Kennedy and Griffin kiss. They couldn't care less that they are in a room full of people right now; all they care about is each other.

"Is that what's wrong? Are you sad that you haven't found someone like Kennedy has?" Lorelei asks softly as we continue to watch Kennedy and Griffin together.

"Yeah, maybe that's it," I admit to her as Kennedy and Griffin say good-bye to everyone and head out on their date.

Or maybe it's the fact that I'm seriously considering fucking up the opportunity Kennedy gave me by going behind her back and starting a new case of my own.

"Paige, you are a sweet, honest person and a great friend. You'll be okay," Lorelei reassures me.

My chest starts to ache as I feel her turn the knife a little deeper into my heart with her words. I thought that by walking away from Matt I would be able to forget about him and his problems. Instead, they followed me home. Even the guilt I feel at

Lorelei's words isn't enough to make me change my mind about what I'm going to do.

As soon as I kissed him, I knew I would help him. I'm sure if I explain to Kennedy that there isn't a case here with Matt being a cheater, we could close it and open up a new one for him so there isn't a conflict of interest. But I know Kennedy won't believe me. She thinks I'm a softie, and she'll just assume I'm taking Matt's side because he's hot, especially since I convinced her she should trust Griffin because that man is sex on a stick. It doesn't matter if I was right; I need to be smart about this.

I need to have solid proof that Melanie is the cheater before I bring Kennedy in.

CHAPTER 5

"Paige, please. You're being unreasonable."

I grit my teeth and try my hardest not to throw the phone against the wall as I sit at my desk and listen to Andy beg. I knew I shouldn't have answered the phone this morning.

"I'm being unreasonable? Are you kidding me with this right now? I'm not giving you any money, Andy. If memory serves me correct, you already have plenty of my money. That's why we're divorced," I remind myself.

Like clockwork, every week for the past month, Andy has called asking for money. He's either extremely desperate, or has the biggest set of balls known to man. And since I was married to him for five years, I know for a fact the latter isn't true.

"I'm not asking for a lot. Just a little bit to tide me over until my bonus from work comes in. I swear I'll pay you back," he pleads.

"Right, like you paid me back the six hundred grand you stole? I don't think so."

"We were husband and wife. It's not stealing. Everything is fifty-fifty when you're married," he reminds me.

"Wow, my math must be really rusty, because you didn't take fifty percent, YOU TOOK IT ALL!"

I'm shouting now. I really hate him for making me lose my temper.

"I wouldn't ask you if it wasn't important. I owe someone money and this person is going to kill me if I don't pay off my debt," Andy explains.

"Yes, I know. You owe me money and I am definitely planning on all the fun ways I'm going to kill you if you don't stop calling me and asking me for money."

Andy sighs on the other end, and I glance down at the notepad in front of me and realize I've written his name and made so many *X*s through it that I've ripped the page to shreds.

"Paige, this is serious. I'm in a lot of trouble here. It's only twenty grand."

Wow, only twenty grand. Sure, no big deal. Let me just bend over and pull it right out of my ass.

"Andy, even if I did have the money, do you really think I'd give it to you? I'm not modeling anymore. I don't have that kind of cash," I remind him.

"I talked to your agent this morning. She said she's been trying to get hold of you about a spread for *InStyle*. That will pay a hundred grand, easy."

The pencil in my hand snaps in half as my anger reaches an all-time high.

"You are such a piece of scum, do you know that? I cannot believe you called Penny. Go to hell, Andy. And stop calling me."

I slam the phone down just as Lorelei walks into the office. She stops in her tracks when she witnesses me lift the receiver and smack it back down over and over until I'm satisfied that the call has ended.

"Let me guess—Andy?"

She walks over to her desk and sets her briefcase on top. I get up from my chair and go over to her as she takes a seat.

"I really don't understand why I married him. Guys like him should be required to wear a sign that says 'I will suck the life out of you,'" I complain.

"How much does he want this time?" Lorelei asks as she pulls a few files out of her briefcase and I perch my hip on the corner of her desk.

"Oh, only twenty thousand dollars. No big deal."

Lorelei laughs and shakes her head. "If he calls again, pass it over to me. I'll use a bunch of big, legal words on him and scare him straight."

I laugh with her and hear the bell ring above the front door, signaling a customer. Craning my head to look over my shoulder, the laughter dies and I let out a gasp. Without even thinking, I dive under Lorelei's desk.

"What the hell are you—"

I smack her leg to make her shut up as she stares under her desk at me with a confused expression on her face.

"Excuse me, I'd like to talk to someone about hiring a private investigator."

I watch from under the desk as Lorelei's head whips up, and I wince as her eyes widen in shock.

"You're Matt Russo," Lorelei whispers.

I smack her leg again and this time, she retaliates by kicking me in the shin. I smack my hand over my mouth to keep the yelp of pain from escaping.

"Um, yeah. How do you know my name?" Matt asks from the other side of the desk.

Oh, my God. This is not happening right now! Shit, shit, shit!

"I'm . . . we just . . . I know . . . " Lorelei flounders and quickly glances under her desk at me. I shrug my shoulders at her in an "I don't know what the fuck is happening right now" gesture. She scoots her chair closer to the desk and I pull my knees up to my chest, making myself as small as possible while holding my breath at the same time.

"I, uh . . . saw a write-up about you in *Graphic Design USA* a while back. Great article," Lorelei states.

This is why she's a big-time attorney and I'm an ex-model, cowering under a desk. She can think on her feet in a crisis.

"Wow! I didn't think anyone even read that magazine," Matt says with a good-natured laugh.

"Oh, yes. I like to keep up-to-date on all the current events in . . . design . . . and graphics. And stuff."

Oh, my God.

"So what can I help you with, Mr. Russo?" Lorelei asks while I listen closely.

"This is so weird. I can't believe I'm even here asking you this, but I need to hire you guys to investigate someone. I've never done anything like this," he explains.

"It was so nice of you to consider Fool Me Once for your investigating needs," Lorelei says quickly. "We're really busy right now, but if you would just leave me your name and number, I'll have someone contact you as soon as possible to let you know if we'll be able to squeeze you into our schedule."

I hear Lorelei slide a piece of paper across the desk and the sounds of Matt scribbling his information and then setting the pen down. "Thanks, I really appreciate it. This is kind of an emergency situation, so I'd like to talk to someone as soon as possible."

Lorelei thanks him again and a few seconds later I hear the ding of the bell as he exits the office. I let out the breath I've been holding and scramble out from under the desk. Lorelei bends over and grabs my arm, hauling me up to my feet.

"What the hell is going on? I thought you said you got the pictures you needed. Why is the man you've been following coming in here to hire us?" Lorelei grills me.

"Are those Jimmy Choos? Are they from the spring collection?" I ask, pointing down to her shoes to try to distract her.

"Oh, these?" she asks, looking down at her feet, taking the bait. "Yes, I just got them yesterday at—PAIGE! Stop it! We can't take him on as a client when we're currently in the middle of trying to catch him cheating. This is the biggest conflict of interest ever! I don't even know why I took down his name and number. I completely panicked. Tell me what's going on, right now!"

Lorelei stomps her foot and I know she means business. I've never seen her lose her temper before. She's as cool and calm as they come, but right now, she looks like she's ready to throttle me.

"So, um, when I trailed him the other night, he recognized me from O'Casey's. We got to talking and, well . . ."

I trail off, trying to come up with a way to make this NOT sound as bad as it is. I've got nothing. The only thing I can do is just blurt it out and hope she doesn't punch me. "I don't think he's cheating on his wife. She's cheating on him and trying to take his family's company because she's a gold-digging whore and I've decided I'm switching teams and I'm going to help him catch her because he seems like a really nice guy and I don't want to see him get hurt."

There. It's done. I take a deep breath after my word vomit and wait for the explosion.

Lorelei is quiet. Too quiet. She just stands here staring at me with her mouth open.

"Say something," I beg her.

Maybe Lorelei will feel my pain. She'll see that this is a matter of importance. She's got a heart buried somewhere in there under all that resentment of her ex-husband.

I look at her imploringly, seeing her face lose its shocked expression.

I knew it! I knew she'd understand.

After a few seconds, Lorelei whispers. "Kennedy is going to kill you."

Well, so much for that idea.

CHAPTER 6

Lorelei was called back into court because a verdict for the case she's working on came in earlier than expected. Thank God for that. If I had to listen to one more minute of her explaining to me all the ways Kennedy would remove the limbs from my body, I was going to scream.

I convinced her not to tell Kennedy by promising I wouldn't do anything stupid until she got back so she could finish raking me over the coals. I wonder if Googling Matt's ex constitutes stupid? It's not like I ran out the door as soon as Lorelei left and went straight to Matt. I'm being smart. I'm doing research. Research doesn't compromise anything.

According to her Facebook page, Melanie Gates-Russo is single. I guess they don't have "whore" as a relationship status. I look through her photo albums and don't see any pictures of her with the mystery man from the other night. She also doesn't have any pictures from her time with Matt. Not that I was looking specifically for pictures of Matt. Like ones of him shirtless. Or sunning himself on a beach. Or lifting weights with sweat dripping down his toned chest.

Research. It's just research.

Melanie certainly has quite a few Internet pictures of kittens in various poses, however. Twenty-two pictures of kittens in sweaters and eighteen of kittens in hats. Seriously? What is she, five?

Clicking out of her photo albums, I notice a status update that wasn't there a few minutes ago:

Hangin' with my grls 2nite at Blu Nightclub. Hit me up!

Are you kidding me with this? He not only married a chick who likes to post kitten pictures, he married one with poor grammar skills. Good God.

Closing out of her Facebook profile, I quickly look up where this Blu Lounge is.

Crap. It's in Indianapolis. That's almost three hours from here.

I glance at the time on my computer. There's no way I can make it there and back before Lorelei gets out of court. She specifically told me to stay put. Taking another few minutes to contemplate what I'm thinking, I shut down my computer and head for the door.

I haven't taken orders from anyone since I left Andy. Why should I start now?

According to its website, Blu is a trendy nightclub in the heart of Indianapolis. Since I had a long drive ahead of me, I ran home, grabbed an appropriate dress, shoved it into my backseat, and changed at a McDonald's right before I got here. As I show my ID to the bouncer, he doesn't even glance at it as he takes in my red, backless halter dress and matching four-inch red peep-toe Steve Madden stilettos before looking at my face. His eyes widen in recognition when he sees who I am, and I smile flirtatiously at him, flustering him a bit so he'll let me in without drawing unwanted attention to myself. I'm immediately assaulted by the thumping beats of Top 40 dance music courtesy of the DJ on the other side of the club. I stick close to the wall as I take in my surroundings.

The dance floor is packed with sweaty, writhing bodies, and all of the VIP lounges around the outer edge of the floor are filled with partiers. I have no idea how I'm ever going to find Melanie in this place, but I have to try.

The VIP areas are all roped off, and you can't even go up the three steps to get to them without an invitation, so I decide to head right through the middle of the dance floor in the hopes that I might spot Melanie.

Five minutes of shoving my way through all of the people, I'm thankful that I pulled my long blonde hair up into a high ponytail. I'm already working up a sweat and I'm not even dancing. With one last surge of my body, I finally make it to the other side and squeeze myself in between a crowd of people standing around the bar.

The bartender hands a drink to the person next to me and then nods his head in my direction. "What can I get you?"

"Just an ice water, please," I shout above the music and loud conversations on either side of me.

While he turns away to grab my drink, I take the time to scan the crowd. This was the dumbest idea I've ever had. There is no way I'm going to find her in this place. There's got to be at least five hundred people here.

"Okay, this is starting to get weird. Are you stalking me?"

My head whips around when I hear the voice close to my ear and I come face-to-face with Matt. I swallow nervously until I see his face light up with a teasing smile. He's not wearing his glasses tonight. Or a sweater vest. Sweet Jesus, does he look good. He's wearing a fitted black button-down with the sleeves pushed up to his elbows tucked into a pair of charcoal-gray dress pants. Gone is nerdy-chic Matt. In his place is hot-as-balls Matt. The temperature in this place suddenly went up a thousand degrees.

"I was just kidding about the stalking thing—don't look so shocked," Matt says with a laugh, right by my ear.

I'm suddenly okay with the noise level in this place if it means he has to be this close to me to talk.

"But seriously, how do we keep showing up at the same places?" he asks again, placing his hand on my hip and pulling me closer to him to make room for a few people trying to get up to the bar.

I'm pressed up against him and staring at his throat while he reaches over to take my glass of ice water from the bartender. I've been around plenty of hot guys before. I've done photo shoots with half-naked male models. None of them has caused this kind of reaction from me. I'm never at a loss for words. Is it because, once again, he caught me doing something that I'm going to lie to him about or because I find myself attracted to him?

"I, um, was in the neighborhood and thought I'd check this place out," I tell him lamely, taking the glass of water from him and sucking down the entire thing.

"You were in the neighborhood? Where exactly do you live? It took me three hours to get here."

I regretfully take a step away from him and set my empty glass on the bar.

"Why are you here?" I ask, taking the focus off of myself.

He sighs and runs his hand through his hair. I suddenly have the urge to do the same with my own hand. I want to clutch his hair and pull his face down to mine so I can feel his lips again.

Holy hell, I need to get this under control. Men suck. They are all pigs, even if they seem nice at first. Andy was really nice at first too. Just because I want to help Matt out and he's easy to look at, doesn't mean anything.

"I found out that Melanie was going to be here tonight. This isn't usually the type of place she goes to, so I was hoping I'd catch her with the guy she's been seeing. I really wish I had a camera on me the other night when we were at Blake's," he says.

I am such a bitch. I could have taken a hundred pictures of Melanie the other night. But in my defense, I didn't know he was the good guy at the time. I hope to God he never finds out about my role in all this.

"Do you think she'll drop everything if you catch her with this guy?" I ask.

"I know she will. Her reputation is important to her. She's all about looking good and making sure everyone thinks she's a saint. If I can catch her and then threaten to out her to her family and mine, she'll back down on the lawsuit. The only problem is, I would never do that to her. Even though our marriage sucked, I could never hurt someone like that. I just hope she doesn't know that."

Oh, God. Why did he have to say that? Why does he have to be such a good guy?

"So, how do you expect to find her in this mess of a place?" I ask, looking around again at all of the people.

"I've already seen her. She's upstairs in one of the VIP lounges," he tells me, pointing over his shoulder to the roped-off area. "I haven't seen any guy with her, though, just a few of her girlfriends."

I look over his shoulder and sure enough, in the very center of the VIP area, in one of the biggest lounges, I see Melanie sitting on a couch with two of her girlfriends on either side of her. They're laughing, toasting, and having a great time.

"Jesus. It's a good thing you're not legally separated yet or all of your alimony would be going right down the drain. Just to sit in that lounge there's a fifteen-hundred-dollar cover charge, plus you have to purchase a minimum of two bottles of top-shelf liquor. In a place like this, that's around nine hundred dollars a bottle," I tell him.

"Wait, how did you know I'm not legally separated yet?"

Oh, no! Oh, shit! I can't really tell him I had Lorelei look that information up for me yesterday, can I?

"Uh, I'm just assuming. You know, since you didn't mention it."

Please let him believe me, please let him believe me.

Matt accepts my lame attempt at an explanation and glances back to Melanie and her friends. "Are you serious that it costs that much to sit in the VIP section? How do you even know that?"

Because I've partied in plenty of those lounges throughout my career. I've hosted parties in those lounges. I could probably tell you the cost and liquor requirements for every club in the United States and the UK.

Something stops me from telling him this, though. Maybe this is the real reason why I have a soft spot for him. He still doesn't know who I am. I'm just a girl he met in a bar. Someone he looks at just like any other normal girl. I want to be normal more than I want to be honest right now and it's killing me.

"I asked when I first got here. You know, just wondering why they had that section roped off," I lie.

He looks back over his shoulder, shaking his head.

"That doesn't make any sense. There is no way in hell she could afford something like that."

I shrug when he turns back to face me. "Maybe one of her friends paid for it."

He shakes his head. "Nope. No way. Melanie is a kindergarten teacher. All of those women she's with? They all teach at the same school she does. They barely make minimum wage."

Well, the multitude of kitten pictures on her Facebook page makes sense now. But I fear for the children of our future if she's the one educating them.

"It has to be the guy she was with the other night then. You don't know anything about him? You didn't recognize him?" I question as someone jostles me from behind and I slam up against the front of Matt.

I put my hands up against his chest and look up at him so I can apologize. He's staring down at me. Actually, he's staring right at my lips and his arms wrap around my waist to steady me, but pull me closer instead.

We stand this way until the noise and all of the people around us fade away like in some cheesy rom-com. All I can focus on is the feel of his body pressed up against mine and the way he can't stop staring at my mouth, like he wants to kiss me.

"This is weird. Is it weird for you? Tell me it's not just me. I mean, I just met you," he explains with frustration.

"It's not just you," I reassure him, feeling equally annoyed and turned on all at the same time.

Shame on me for thinking I was going to get out of this with my heart intact.

CHAPTER 7

"A re you sure? I don't have a good feeling about this," Matt tells me as he grips my hand tightly while I pull him with me through the dance floor and over to the roped-off VIP area.

I stop right at the edge of the dance floor and turn around to face him. "I'm sure. Don't worry. Someone needs to go up there and get her to talk, and it's obviously not going to be you. She has no idea who I am, so it's the perfect plan."

He glances back and forth between the VIP area and me. "You must think I'm a complete loser. What kind of guy asks the most beautiful woman in this place to spy on his ex-wife?"

I laugh and rub my hand up and down his arm reassuringly. "You didn't ask. I volunteered. But thank you for the compliment."

"I don't know why I'm even worrying. You're never going to be able to get in there," he tells me, staring at the bald, buff, badass-looking bouncer who is currently standing guard in front of the ropes.

"Don't worry about me, I'm pretty resourceful," I tell him with a wink. "Just wait for me back by the bar so she doesn't see you."

He leans in and kisses me on the cheek before walking away. I watch him push his way back through the crowd, then I take a deep breath and walk right up to the bouncer, tapping him on the shoulder so he'll look down at me.

He turns his head with a scowl on his face, not too happy about the fact that yet another person is going to bug him to get up into the VIP area. When he sees me standing there, the scowl turns into a huge smile that appears rather strange on a man who looks like he just got out of prison.

"Paige! Holy shit! What the fuck are you doing slumming here, beautiful?"

Yet another thing I failed to mention to Matt—I recognized the bouncer as soon as I walked into the club. He was one of the regular bouncers at a club I frequented during the height of my modeling career.

"Ronny, it's so good to see you!" I tell him as he leans down and scoops me up into a bone-crushing hug, lifting me up off of my feet.

I guess when you're six foot seven and weigh over three hundred pounds, you could lift a building without breaking a sweat.

Ronny finally sets me back on my feet and holds me out at arm's length.

"When did you start working here? Last time I saw you, you were breaking up a fight at the Viper Room in LA," I remind him.

"Eh, the wife got transferred to Indy for her job. So here I am," he says with a shrug. "You want to go up into the VIP area?"

He nods behind him and unhooks one end of the velvet rope.

"Thanks, Ronny. Give Kim my love," I tell him as I walk past him and into the private area.

"Will do. Don't be a stranger now," he calls after me, hooking the rope back into place after I walk through.

I make my way up the three steps to the walkway that leads to all of the VIP lounges, grabbing a glass of champagne off of a passing tray as a waiter walks by. I pause just outside of the wall of Melanie's lounge and take a deep breath.

Showtime.

Putting on a huge smile, I giggle at nothing as I stumble into the opening of the room and flop down on the end of the huge sectional sofa where Melanie and her friends are sitting. They immediately stop talking and stare at me. They look like Charlie's Angels. Melanie in the middle is blonde, the friend on her left is a brunette, and the one on her right has black hair.

"Oh, my gosh! I'm SO drunk. I'm totally in the wrong lounge!" I tell them with another giggle and a sip of my champagne.

They immediately smile at me and Melanie speaks first. "It's cool. Drink up, sister!"

She raises her glass and her three friends copy her, all of them taking a sip of their drinks. I notice two bottles of Dos Lunas Grand Reserve tequila sitting on the table in front of them and even I'm shocked by the indulgence I see right now. Just one of those bottles is easily twenty-two hundred dollars. Whoever booked this room isn't playing around.

Time to get to the bottom of things.

"I hope you don't mind me hiding out in here for a minute. The guy who invited me to his lounge is a total creeper," I complain with a roll of my eyes.

"We don't mind at all!" the brunette next to Melanie speaks up. "There are a lot of creeps here tonight. Thank God we're in here and not out there."

She points out to the dance floor and the rest of the girls nod in agreement.

"Are you guys hiding out too? Wait, did you guys pay for this room yourself? You must be, like, totally rich or something," I say with wide, innocent eyes.

"Oh, hell no! We could never afford something like this. Melanie has a rich boyfriend!" the brunette says with a laugh.

Melanie shushes her and the other friend smacks the brunette in the arm. All three of them look over at me nervously.

"Sorry, it's just . . . I'm not really supposed to talk about him," Melanie tells me.

What the hell?

"Is he a spy or something?" I ask with a laugh.

"No. He's, um . . . a businessman. He's just very private."

Right. My ass he's just a businessman.

No one says anything for a few seconds and then the brunette finally rolls her eyes and laughs. "Oh, what the hell, Melanie. What's the point of dating him if you can't brag about it?"

Melanie sighs and then looks around. When she's satisfied that no one is walking by the room, possibly listening in, she shrugs and nods to her friend.

"She's totally dating someone in the Mob!" the brunette gushes. "Like in *The Godfather*, but cooler!"

Oh, no. This is not good. Maybe they only THINK he's in the Mob. They don't seem very bright. Maybe they misunderstood.

"He's got more money than God, I swear," the one with the black hair finally adds.

Melanie is still keeping quiet about the boyfriend. I need to turn up the drunk-moron routine if I want her to tell me what I need to know. I can't really go back to the office and Google "members of the Mob."

"Wow, that must be so awesome. My ex was a total loser. He had a bunch of money, but never spent any of it on me," I complain.

That's all it takes. Melanie's eyes light up and she looks at me like we're long-lost sisters.

"Oh, my gosh, me too! My ex practically owned his own company and he wouldn't even consider buying a summer home in the Hamptons when I asked him," Melanie whines. "Vinnie buys me stuff every day and takes me to all the best restaurants. He's a total keeper. But just in case, I'm still going to take my ex for all he has."

All three of the girls laugh and clink their glasses together.

I want to punch this bitch right in her selfish little face.

"So, this guy is really in the Mob? Like, the real Mob?" I ask.

"He totally is! He's like the boss or something. But you can't tell anyone I told you this, okay?" she begs.

Yeah. Right. Your secret is safe with me.

I sit with the girls for a few more minutes as they all go on and on about how amazing this Vinnie person is because he isn't afraid to shell out thousands of dollars a day on Melanie, and how Matt isn't going to know what hit him when she takes control of the company.

It's sad and pathetic and makes me even more determined to do whatever I can to help Matt. I also make a mental note to never send any future children I might have to the school system these idiots work for.

Unfortunately, none of them are forthcoming with Vinnie's last name and I find out that he's not joining them tonight because he had some business to take care of. If he really is with the Mob, I'm going to go out on a limb here and assume this "business" probably has something to do with offing someone. I might make a few stupid choices here and there, but even I know that trying to hunt down someone who works for the Mob just to get a few pictures of him with Melanie is a bad idea. I'm going to have to come up with another plan for making sure Melanie keeps her greedy paws off of Matt's company.

CHAPTER 8

No. Absolutely not. There is no way you are going to dig deeper into this guy's background. That just has bad news written all over it," I tell Matt.

After we left the club, we decided to stop at a twenty-four-hour diner on the way home. Since we drove separately to the club, Matt followed me in his car.

"What else am I supposed to do? You said it yourself: She is determined to fuck me over. I can't let that happen, Paige."

Reaching across the table, I rest my hands on top of his. "I know. We'll think of something else. I have a few contacts in law enforcement. Let me have them do some checking first and find out what we're dealing with."

Matt stares at me across the table and I can't bring myself to move my hands off of his even when the waitress comes over and refills our coffee cups. I think back to his words at the club about this thing between us being weird. It is weird, but in a good way. I feel like I've known him forever.

"Where did you even come from? My life was total shit a week ago and then all of a sudden, you show up out of nowhere and make everything better," he tells me with a smile.

I swallow past the lump in my throat. Now would be the perfect opportunity to tell him that it wasn't a coincidence, me showing up in his life the way I did.

"You are amazing," Matt tells me earnestly.

I shake my head at him, wishing the words would come out of my mouth as easily as they pop into my head.

"Yes, you are," he insists. "I barely know anything about you, but I know that much at least. I'm pretty much a stranger to you and yet you're willing to do whatever you can to help me out. That's amazing, if you ask me."

Oh, but you aren't a stranger, Matt. I've read your file. I've MEMORIZED your file.

"So, tell me something about you. I've bored you to death and most likely insulted the hell out of you with my problems. What do you do for a living when you aren't trying to make it in the modeling world?" he asks, moving one of his hands out from under mine to pick up his coffee cup and bring it to his lips.

Of course he couldn't start with something easy, like my favorite color.

"I've actually given up the modeling dream. Um, I mostly just do some office work for my best friend's company."

I am going straight to hell.

"Why would you give up on the modeling thing? You're gorgeous, obviously. I have a hard time believing it wouldn't be a pretty lucrative career for you once you got your foot in the door."

If you only knew . . .

"I just realized it wasn't something I loved doing. It got old really fast," I explain, giving him as much as I can of myself right now. A part of me wants to tell him everything. About how I was, and still am, kind of a big deal in the modeling world. How I got tired of being paraded around in front of people for my looks, no one even considering that I might have a brain that I'd want to use for something else. And how the person I loved, trusted, and married only cared about my looks and used me for what those looks provided him. It's so refreshing being anonymous that I'm almost drunk from the joy it brings me.

"You should never do something you're not passionate about. I'm glad you aren't doing it anymore if it didn't make you happy. Although it would have been kind of cool to drive down Route 20 and see your picture splashed across a billboard," he jokes before taking another sip of his coffee.

Well, it's a good thing we're not taking Interstate 69 home, then, since there is currently one of me at mile marker seventy-two modeling a bathing suit for Victoria's Secret.

I laugh uncomfortably as I watch him drink his coffee. I can't do this anymore. I want to be honest with him. He's poured his heart out to me and I sit here and continue to lie to him. He needs to know where I work, and he needs to know that I know everything about Melanie.

"Matt, I need to tell you—"

"Paige, what the hell is going on?"

Jerking my hand away from Matt's, I stare up in shock at Andy standing next to our table, staring down at us with an annoyed look on his face. He's wearing his usual work attire: a black suit with an interchangeable shirt and tie in various colors. He's wearing blue right now, so it must be Friday. Andy is the most anal person I've ever met, but something is going on with him. He's a hot mess right now. Instead of his typical clean-cut, perfectly pressed appearance, he looks like he hasn't slept in days, or if he has, he's slept in his clothes. He's a wrinkled disaster and I have never seen him with so much facial hair. He was always meticulous about shaving every single morning.

"Andy? What are you doing here?" I demand.

"I didn't like how our last conversation ended. You didn't answer my calls this afternoon and I got worried," he explains, with a dirty look at Matt.

"So you followed me? Are you insane? GO HOME, Andy."

Andy ignores me and continues to stare at Matt. "Who are you?"

Matt looks back and forth between us before sliding out of his seat and standing up in front of Andy.

How did I ever think that the two of them were anything alike? Seeing the two of them side by side, the differences are glaringly obvious. Andy is short, whiny, and annoying. Matt is easily five inches taller than he is, and working in an office all day hasn't diminished his intimidation skills in the least. I watch in awe as Matt stares Andy down and Andy visibly shrinks into himself and takes a step back.

"My name's Matt, and I'm a friend of Paige's. I think it would be best if you do as she says and go home," he tells Andy in a calm voice.

Andy gets a sudden second wind of self-confidence and puffs out his chest, stepping around Matt and up to my side. "Look, I talked to Penny again. She said you still have plenty of time to say yes to the *InStyle* photo shoot. The mag has even upped their original offer—a hundred and fifty grand and the promise of the cover. It's their anniversary issue and they really want you for it."

Pushing myself up out of the bench seat, I get right into Andy's face. "I already told you this earlier. I'm not doing this just to pay off your debt. I'm done modeling, Andy. Get that through your head."

Andy crosses his arms over his chest and huffs at me. "You're being childish, Paige. You're one of the top models in the entire country. You've been in every fucking magazine they print in the US and CoverGirl wants you to do another commercial. You don't just up and quit something like that for some silly pipe dream of being a private investigator."

"Shut up, Andy. Shut up right now," I warn him, refusing to look over at Matt.

"I think it's time for you to leave," Matt tells Andy through clenched teeth as he steps in between us.

Luckily, the waitress rushes over to check on us before I pick up my fork from the table and stab it into Andy's smug face.

"Is everything okay here? Do I need to get the manager?" she asks, glancing back and forth between the three of us.

"Oh no, there's no need for that. Everything is fine. He was just leaving," I state, staring angrily at Andy.

Andy huffs and turns away from me to look at Matt. "Maybe you can talk some sense into her. She's never going to amount to anything at that stupid, man-hating Fool Me Once Investigations. The only thing she's good for is sitting there and looking pretty."

Andy barely finishes his tirade before Matt's fist connects with his face. Andy's head whips back with the force of the blow, and he immediately starts screaming like a girl.

"OH, MY GOD! I THINK YOU BROKE MY NOSE!"

Andy is bent over at the waist, holding both of his hands over his nose as the blood drips down his fingers and onto the floor by his feet.

"Get the fuck out of here before I break something else of yours," Matt growls at him.

I'm pretty sure my underwear just spontaneously combusted.

Andy finally gets the hint and scurries out of the restaurant without another word, whimpering the entire way out the door. After he's gone, Matt turns around to face me.

"I think I should probably tell you, that was the hottest thing I've ever seen," I admit to him.

"Stop. Just . . . stop."

I shut my mouth and quickly realize that now is not the time for jokes. Even if I'm not joking at all. I really want to throw him down on the ground and rip his clothes off.

"A little modeling? You must think I'm a complete idiot," Matt says softly.

I shake my head frantically back and forth. "No! It's nothing like that, I swear."

"You HAVE been following me, haven't you? Jesus Christ, is anything about you even true? Did Melanie hire you?"

He waits for me to argue, but I have nothing to say. Not one word.

"She did, didn't she? Fuck! This entire time, you've been playing me for a fool. I really am an idiot," he mutters angrily.

"Matt, please. Just let me explain," I plead.

"I think I've had enough explanations for one night. Tell my ex I hope she enjoys the company."

Matt turns and storms out of the restaurant, slamming the door open so hard it bangs against the outside of the building.

"So, you ready for the check now?" the waitress deadpans.

I flop down into the booth and stare longingly out the front door.

Well, so much for this night ending with another amazing kiss.

CHAPTER 9

On Sunday morning, there's a knock at my door and I contemplate ignoring it. I haven't showered in two days. I'm facedown on my couch, where I've been since I got home Friday night. At least I changed out of my dress when I got home that night. Too bad I haven't changed out of the Hello Kitty pajama bottoms and tank top I put on after I ripped off my dress and threw it in the trash. I feel gross. But I deserve to feel gross. I suck.

There's another knock at the door, this one louder than the first. I don't even lift my head from the cushion or move my body. They'll go away eventually.

"PAIGE McCARTY, OPEN UP THIS DOOR RIGHT NOW OR I'M GOING TO KICK IT DOWN!" Kennedy yells.

Shit. Kennedy will never go away. And she really will kick my door down. I've seen her do it before.

With a sigh, I push myself up from the couch and shuffle my feet over to the door, opening it up while Kennedy continues to pound on it with her fist.

"Jesus Christ, you look like shit," Kennedy tells me as she pushes her way into my condo.

"Well, aren't you just a ray of sunshine this morning," I deadpan as I close the door behind her and go right back to my previous position on the couch.

I know why she's here. Aside from the fact that I've been ignoring her since Friday night, I'm positive that Matt called the office and filled her in on what a lying bitch I am. She's probably here to fire me. I'm an ex-model and now an ex-almost-private investigator. I'm washed up. A has-been. They're going to do an *E! True Hollywood Story* on me and it's going to be depressing.

"Care to tell me why you haven't answered my or Lorelei's calls in the past two days?" Kennedy asks.

"Don't feel bad about firing me. I already know I screwed up," I mumble into the couch.

"*Drph feem brph amerph frmy meh. Eh affreffy mow eh srphed upff*" is what Kennedy hears.

Kennedy's hand slides under my face and she lifts my head up off of the cushion. "You want to try that again? I don't speak couch cushion."

I sigh, pushing myself up, and move to the middle, flopping back down on my butt this time. I repeat the part about firing me.

Kennedy stares down at me. "What the hell are you talking about? Why would I fire you?"

Either she has no clue what I'm referring to, or she's just messing with me. I wouldn't put it past her. Maybe she wants me to die a slow, painful death of humiliation.

"You know, the whole Matt Russo thing," I add, fishing for clues that she knows what I've done.

Kennedy shakes her head at me in annoyance. "So you haven't been able to catch the bastard cheating yet. It's not that big of a deal, Paige. Just give it time."

Oh, my God. He didn't call and tell her everything. Wait. Why didn't he call and tell her everything?

"I know I'm not hip to fashion like you are, but you do know you're wearing Hello Kitty pants, right?" she asks, staring down at my legs.

"Did you just say 'hip to fashion'? What are you, ninety?"

"Oh, fuck off. Get your ass up and take a shower. Do you want to . . . go shoe shopping or something?" Kennedy asks, visibly wincing when she says the word "shopping."

"Awww, it's so sweet that you would do that just to make me feel better," I tell her with a smile. "There's a sale at Nordstrom today and I want to swing by a few salons so we can interview new stylists, since ours became a drug runner. We should also get you some new lingerie to make Griffin happy, and there's this black dress I want your opinion on at Express."

I watch the horror come over her face with each and every word I say, and I feel a little less sorry for myself as I tease her.

"Wipe that look off your face. Like I'd really put you through all that torture in one day," I tell her.

"Thank Christ."

Now that she sees I'm still alive and not planning on forcing her to shop with me all day, Kennedy turns and heads for the door. "Lorelei said you might have gotten a few photos the other night that you think aren't good enough to nail Matt. Upload them onto my computer when you get to the office tomorrow and I'll take a look."

Well, shit. Now I really AM going to cry. Lorelei didn't rat me out to Kennedy either. Now I just need to think of a way to "lose" those photos and find out who this Vinnie guy is before Kennedy realizes I have completely violated the contract she signed with Melanie. Knowing that gold-digging whore, she'll come back and sue us too.

❦

"So, I know you didn't just ask me to lunch because you miss me. What's the real reason I'm here?" Ted asks me.

Ted was recently promoted to detective with the South Bend Police Department after he assisted Kennedy in bringing down one of the biggest drug rings in Indiana a few weeks ago. He mostly works with the DEA, but I know he's got the inside scoop on pretty much every criminal in this state.

"Of course I miss you. I feel like we haven't hung out in ages," I lie.

"I wasn't born yesterday, Paige. What are you up to and does Kennedy know about it?" he asks.

I bristle at his comment that Kennedy needs to know everything I'm doing. Once again, people misjudge my ability to get anything done on my own.

"I'm working on my own case and no, Kennedy doesn't know about it. Not yet. I want to get some more concrete information before I go to her."

The lies are just flowing right off my tongue these days.

"Don't you just handle office work and stuff?"

"Contrary to popular belief, I'm not an idiot. I do have a brain, and every once in a while, I like to use it," I reply cockily.

"That's not what I meant and you know it. I just want to make sure you're being safe. My sister has a lot of experience taking down bad guys and even she was an idiot with how she handled things a few weeks ago."

"I'm not taking down any bad guys, I promise. I just need information on one," I admit.

"You swear you aren't going to go off half-cocked like she did and go to some nut job's house alone?" Ted asks.

I raise my right hand. "I swear."

Ted sighs and shakes his head at me. "Fine. Give me his name."

I lift up my knife and fork and begin cutting up my salad. "His name is Vinnie and he might be some sort of Mob boss."

Ted doesn't answer me and I stop my cutting to look up at him. He's staring at me with his mouth open. "What?"

"Tell me you aren't talking about Vinnie DeMarco."

I shrug my shoulders. "I don't know. Am I talking about Vinnie DeMarco? I only got his first name."

"Paige, whatever you're doing—stop. You do not want to go fishing around in Vinnie DeMarco's life, trust me. He is bad news," Ted warns me.

"How bad are we talking? *The Godfather* bad or *The Sopranos* bad?" I ask.

"Is there a fucking difference? They all do whatever the hell they want and don't care about who they hurt in the process. We've been trying to nail this guy for years, but he's slippery. He hires people to do everything for him so he never gets his hands dirty. And the people he hires are extremely devoted. They'll do life in prison before they give him up. And if they even think about ratting him out, no one ever hears from them again."

I take a minute to process this information. If this is the Vinnie that Melanie is seeing, it's even worse than I thought. Matt isn't going to be able to just snap a photo of them and threaten her with it. He'll get himself killed. I need to be smart about this.

"Have you heard anything about this Vinnie guy having a girlfriend?" I ask next.

"He's got a hundred different girlfriends all over the US. Who knows who his flavor of the week is nowadays," Ted informs me, picking up his burger and taking a huge bite.

I should probably tell him that I might know who his latest conquest is. It might help them bring this guy down, but for right now, I'm keeping this information to myself. I need to make sure Melanie isn't a threat to Matt before I do anything. If she's called in and questioned, it could just piss her off and make her even more vindictive.

"I'm serious, Paige. You stay as far away from Vinnie DeMarco as possible. And if you hear anything, and I mean anything, you tell me right away," Ted warns.

I smile brightly at him and dig into my salad. "Cross my heart."

Shame on me for making a promise on a heart that barely functions anymore.

CHAPTER 10

"He was a really great guy. He was nice and pretty and . . . nice . . ." I trail off as I stare into my wineglass.

"You already said 'nice.'"

I look up at the bartender and scowl. "Aren't bartenders supposed to be friendly and helpful? Stop judging me and bring me more wine."

The bartender walks away and I put my elbow on top of the bar, resting my head on my hand. Sliding my phone across the bar closer to myself, I stare at the blank screen. I double-check the 3G icon at the top to make sure my phone is still working. I feel like I'm in high school again, bringing the receiver of our house phone up to my ear every ten minutes to make sure there was still a dial tone.

It's been five days since I last saw Matt and four days since I sent him a pathetic text apologizing for lying to him.

And four days since he never replied to my stupid text.

The bartender sets another glass of Moscato in front of me and scurries away, probably afraid I'm going to start crying again. I don't blame him. I'm pitiful. Since when did I become the type of woman who sits around for days on end waiting for a text from a guy and then imbibes way too much wine to make the pain go away?

I'll tell you when—when Matt Russo walked into my life.

Okay, fine. I did it with Asshole Andy, but I thought I'd learned my lesson since then. I'd been fine all these months being alone. I was perfectly okay with the fact that I was finally becoming the strong, independent woman I wanted to be. Now I'm sitting at a bar alone downing drinks and staring at my phone, willing it to send me a text from him.

I tried to keep myself busy since I sent him that text. I deleted the incriminating photos of the two of us kissing off of Lorelei's camera when she was in court so Kennedy would never see them. Looking through those pictures and seeing his lips on me, remembering how they felt, just depressed me even more.

I did some Google searches on Vinnie DeMarco and talked to Ted again in the hopes that he would give me more information on the guy aside from "He's mean and scary and you should stay far away from him." The only thing he let slip was that there is a current investigation of the guy being handled by the criminal investigations unit. Something about an illegal gambling ring and stolen property reports leading back to the members. Obviously it's nothing that will help me prove that Melanie is a cheater. I want so bad to be able to do this for Matt, and the fact that I keep striking out has made me depressed.

I hate that he thinks I'm a liar and that nothing about me was true and honest. I had hoped my text to him would make him realize that I was trying to make things right. Obviously I was wrong. He wants nothing to do with me and I don't blame him.

Picking up my chilled glass of wine, I chug it and clumsily smack the empty glass down on the bar. When it looks like the bar tips sideways like the *Titanic* going under, I realize sucking down that glass probably wasn't the best idea.

My cell phone vibrates and bounces up and down on top of the bar. It takes a few tries before I can get my six hands to grab onto it and see on the display that it's Lorelei calling.

Wait, I don't have six hands, do I? This vibration feels funny. I should stick it down my pants and pretend it's Matt.

"Hey, hang up and call me again so I can pretend it's Matt in my pants," I answer with a giggle.

"Oh, my God, are you drunk?" Lorelei asks through the line.

I can hear the annoyance in her voice. Lorelei never gets drunk. Lorelei wouldn't understand my need to get drunk and forget I ever met Matt Russo.

"I'm not drunk, I'm hammered," I tell her with a snort.

"Where are you? I'm coming to get you."

"HEY! BARTENDER!" I yell, pulling the phone away from my ear. He stops stacking glasses behind the bar and walks over to me.

"I don't think you need a refill," he deadpans.

"Oh, you're a funny, funny little man. Where are we?"

He stares at me like I'm an idiot. Screw him! I'm not a drunk; I'm just an idiot. Wait, no. I'm not a drunk; I'm an idiot.

Shit! I'm so drunk.

"This is Mulligan's. It says so on the glass in front of you. And on the napkin underneath it. And hey, even on this giant neon sign right above my head," he tells me sarcastically, pointing above him.

Smartass. I blow a raspberry at him like the mature adult I am and hear the faint sound of Lorelei yelling through the phone.

"DON'T GO ANYWHERE! I'll be there in ten minutes."

<hr />

"Did you see that? A light just went on!" I tell Lorelei excitedly.

As soon as Lorelei dragged me out of Mulligan's with an apology to the bartender for my behavior, she shoved me into her sleek black Mercedes with a firm warning not to puke on her leather upholstery. We left my car in the parking lot and Lorelei promised to bring me back the next day to pick it up. Somewhere between the bar and my condo, I convinced her we needed to go to Matt's house because it was a matter of life or death.

Let it never be said that "ex-models turned private investigators" can't act. Even with seven glasses of wine in their systems.

"Amazing. He has electricity," Lorelei answers, her voice void of emotion.

We're currently parked right out front of Matt's house. As soon as we pulled up and Lorelei killed the engine, I tried to convince her that we could better assess the situation from a closer vantage point, say in his bushes, but she immediately vetoed my idea. She muttered something about crazy drunk women and how her colleagues would hang their head in shame at her for listening to me, but I tuned her out. All I cared about was getting a glimpse of him. Just one little peek.

I press my nose against the passenger-side window and spot Matt walking through his living room wearing just a pair of pajama bottoms. He scratches his muscled chest as he walks past the window and disappears from sight.

Never before have I ever wanted to be a hand more than I do right now. Who knew he was packing all of that heat underneath his button-down shirts?

"I cannot believe you convinced me to do this," Lorelei complains for the tenth time since we pulled up. "Remind me again why we're parked outside Matt Russo's house in the middle of the night? Because right now, I am not buying your story that you think he's in danger. Stop drooling on my window."

I pull my face away from the glass and turn to face her. She's not happy with me. I sort of don't blame her. I'm not happy with myself either now that the alcohol buzz has begun to fade. I may or may not have told a little white lie to convince Lorelei to take a detour on the way to my condo. There might have been a mention of someone stalking Matt, and I might have told her it was the Mob and that they all carry guns and his life could be on the line. And since I'm being honest, I might as well admit that I threatened to throw myself out of her car into oncoming traffic if she didn't bring me here immediately. In my defense, it was the booze that did all of the talking for me.

Okay. Fine. A little bit of my heart as well. But mostly the booze.

"I just wanted to make sure he was okay. He hasn't been happy lately," I mumble, turning away from her just in time to see Matt's living room window go dark, and I sigh dejectedly that I didn't get another look at him.

"How do you know he hasn't been happy lately if this is the first time you've seen him since last week when he stormed out of the diner?"

I wince and slowly turn back to face her. I couldn't keep the guilty look off my face if I tried.

Lorelei's eyes widen and her jaw drops. "Oh, my God! The Mob isn't stalking him, YOU'RE stalking him!" she shouts.

"SHHHHHHH! He might hear you!" I whisper. My head whips around and I stare in horror at his front door, expecting him to come bursting out of it any minute and charge over to the car, demanding to know why I'm out here watching him. Actually, now that I think about it, that might not be a bad thing. I'd be able to see his naked chest up close and personal.

"Paige, I highly suggest you never drink again. People make utterly unhealthy life choices when they drink and this just proves it. It's one o'clock in the morning and we're parked outside a man's house because you have some misplaced affection for him."

"It's not misplaced. I know exactly where it is," I tell her stubbornly, crossing my arms in front of me.

"You've been stalking him all week, haven't you?" Lorelei demands.

It's like she KNOWS I followed him to work once.

Okay, three times. I just wanted to make sure the anger and irritation I saw flashed across his face that first time wasn't a fluke.

And it wasn't. Each time I saw him this past week he looked exactly the same. Like he would punch anyone who rubbed him the wrong way. I felt responsible for putting that look on his face.

"Will you stop calling it 'stalking'? That's such a harsh term. I prefer 'anonymous following.'"

She clenches her jaw and narrows her eyes at me.

"What is this really about? Is it because Andy won't leave you alone about the money? Are you just latching yourself onto the first decent guy who comes along to make him jealous or something? This isn't like you, Paige."

Letting my head thump back against the headrest, I close my eyes and sigh. She's right. This isn't like me.

"It has absolutely nothing to do with Andy. I couldn't care less if he's jealous. I just . . . I don't want to end up like my mother. Seventy years old, bitter, and alone."

It's the first time I've ever admitted anything like this, and honestly, I didn't even know it bothered me until I found someone like Matt and then lost him before it even had a chance to go anywhere.

"And who says you will? You're the only one who has the power over your own life, Paige. YOU control your destiny. I'll admit, I don't like the idea that we're sitting outside of this guy's house stalk—"

I cut her off with a glare and she huffs in annoyance.

"Anonymously following. I think you're insane for not telling Kennedy that you've strayed from the original investigation, but I guess I understand," Lorelei tells me softly. "It's difficult watching Kennedy and Griffin be so in love and not have the same thing for ourselves."

This little piece of sincerity from Lorelei shocks me into stunned silence. Lorelei has always been adamant about never wanting to fall in love again. She swore off men for the rest of her life because she doesn't think love is worth the hassle.

It completely throws me that underneath the tough exterior of hers there's a mushy romantic just like me.

"Can we please just go home so you can sleep off the booze emanating from your pores? All of this honesty tonight makes me want to castrate Andy AND Matt for messing with your heart."

Okay, maybe not THAT mushy.

"Will you promise not to judge me for the poor choices I made while intoxicated?" I beg.

Lorelei starts up the car and pulls away from the curb. "I promise. I'll even help you figure out a way to get Matt to forgive you, if that's what you really want. One that doesn't involve anonymous following or calling a bartender a dick."

"I should probably go back and apologize for that, huh?"

CHAPTER 11

Without bothering to remove the dark sunglasses perched on my face, I slide into the church pew at Saint Michael's and briefly wonder if God knows I came into his house smelling like booze and shame.

"Take your glasses off—this isn't a disco," my mother whispers harshly in my ear.

Thankfully, I roll my eyes at her before I remove them. And avoid reminding her that it's no longer 1970.

"Care to enlighten me on why you asked me to meet you at church?" I ask as I wince at the bright sunlight streaming through the stained-glass windows while I stuff my sunglasses into my purse.

"You mean aside from the fact that your soul needs saving and it's been over a month since you've set foot into a church?" she whispers back.

Super. Hangover from hell AND an extra helping of guilt.

I raise my eyebrow at her as the organ music blasts from behind us. She immediately stands and begins singing along with the other parishioners, ignoring me completely.

I wait for the song to end and everyone to sit back down before I try again.

"What was so important that it couldn't wait until later today?" I whisper.

She shushes me when the priest begins talking, and it takes everything in me not to loudly remind her that she chose this meeting spot. After a few minutes, she leans in closer to me.

"Someone stole the Communion hosts from the church last week. And yesterday, the gold chalice went missing. You need to tell your friend Kennedy to help us."

I bristle a little at the fact that she didn't demand that I help her solve this case. She's convinced my only purpose at Fool Me Once is to be a whore. Even my own mother doesn't believe in my abilities.

"You know I work there too, right? Why couldn't I be the one to help you?"

Not that I would. I'm too busy right now failing to help Matt, but it's the principle of the thing.

"You kiss strange men and take nudie pictures. How are you going to help us?"

No matter how many times I tell her that kissing those men is a way for me to catch them cheating or how tasteful the photos are that I've done, she knows someone whose best friend goes to this church who has a daughter who posed for *Playboy* and then went on to do porn, or something like that. As soon as I was hired for my first modeling job ten years ago, she started praying the rosary every single night because she thought she'd lost me to the dark side.

"They aren't nudie pictures. How many times do I have to tell you this?" I whisper angrily.

She shushes me again.

"We're in the Lord's house. This isn't the time to be talking about your boo-boos," she informs me, her hands waving in the general direction of my boobs.

I love my mother. I love my mother. I love my mother. Maybe if I keep reminding myself, I won't strangle her in a church full of people.

The organ music starts up again and everyone stands.

"Mom, we're a little busy at work right now. Why doesn't someone just call the police and report the theft?"

She frowns at me. "That chalice was a gift from the Pope."

She quickly crosses herself at the mention of the Pope and I roll my eyes.

My mother was born and raised Catholic and she had a very strict upbringing. When she left for college, she sowed her wild oats and went a little crazy. She never settled down and by the time she was forty, she had given up on ever finding Mr. Right and having a family. Fate decided to give her a nice swift kick in the ass on her fortieth birthday, however.

My mother was . . . how do I put this nicely . . . basically, my mother was a cougar. On her birthday, she decided to celebrate with a few girlfriends at a local college bar. After too many shots of whiskey, she met my father. He was a college student from the University of Michigan, visiting a few of his friends at Notre Dame for the weekend. Wham, bam, thank you, ma'am, and six weeks later, the stick turned pink. She never got my dad's name and was too mortified to ever go back to the bar and ask around about him.

My mother immediately went back to her Catholic-guilt roots and started going to confession and Mass every single day. At seventy years old, she continues to go to Mass every day, I'm sure to pray for my soul, which she assumes is indecent and always naked.

"See that nice young man two rows in front of us with the blue shirt? That's Harold Johnson. He's single and his mother told me he's always had a crush on you."

I don't even bother looking at the man in question. Ever since Andy and I got divorced, she's been trying to set me up with random men at church.

"You're kidding, right? His name is Harry Johnson?" I whisper back, trying to contain my laughter.

"What's wrong with his name? It's a strong Christian name," she argues.

"That's not a strong Christian name. It's a name that shouts 'my parents hate me.'"

"He has a good job and he even takes care of his mother," she replies, ignoring my barb.

"Takes care of her, or lives in her basement?"

She huffs in irritation. "There is nothing wrong with a forty-year-old man living with his poor, ailing mother. You're not getting any younger, Paige. You need to find someone special."

"How do you know I haven't found someone special?" I demand.

She pulls her head away and stares at me, searching my face to see if I'm being honest. I've never been able to lie to my mother and she knows it. Even in high school when I thought I could get away with anything because she was always gone from the house doing one thing or another for the church. Five minutes in the door and she'd be able to figure out just by looking at me how many beers I snuck at a party when I was supposed to be studying.

"Maybe I've already found a great guy," I mumble, sniffling in sadness.

"You'll never find a great guy if you continue working as a floozy," she counters.

"Oh, my God, I am not a floozy! I haven't had sex with anyone since Andy!"

Of course the church chooses that moment to go completely silent. My mother looks around frantically and smiles embarrassedly to the people within hearing distance.

"At least wait until after Communion to talk about *s-e-x*," she scolds in my ear, spelling out the word like I'm a toddler.

I make it through the rest of Mass without doing my mother any bodily harm and as we exit the church, she walks me up to the priest.

"Beautiful sermon today, Father Bob. You remember my daughter, Paige?"

Father Bob shakes my hand and gives me a warm smile. "Of course I remember her. It's been a while since I've seen you at Mass."

My mother looks pointedly at me and I immediately feel like I'm in second grade at confession for the first time and quickly drop Father Bob's hand.

Forgive me, Father, for I have sinned. It's been a month since my last church service and I've been having impure thoughts.

"My mother mentioned you've had problems lately with some thefts in the church. I'm not sure if she told you, but I work for a private investigations firm," I tell him, quickly shutting down my brain and thoughts of being impure with Matt.

"Oh, yes, yes. It's really not as bad as it sounds. I'm positive it's just some poor, homeless soul who has strayed from the path of God. All we need to do is say some prayers and everything will be fine."

Father Bob quickly excuses himself before I can reply and rushes away to greet other parishioners.

I watch him silently for a few minutes and every once in a while he looks back over his shoulder at me, turning away quickly when he catches me staring.

"Father Bob looks guilty. I think he knows more than he's letting on," I tell my mother as we make our way to the parking lot.

"Paige Elizabeth! Father Bob is a saint. That man baptized you, gave you your First Holy Communion, and married you and Andy," she admonishes.

"Yeah, and we see how well that turned out," I mutter.

"Fran, Eunice, come over here and say hello to Paige."

I turn in the direction my mother is looking and see her two friends quickly amble over to us. Well, as quickly as they can considering Fran uses a cane and Eunice is pushing a walker.

"Paige, it's good to see you back at church. Did you hear that Harold Johnson is single?" Eunice asks.

Oh, for the love of God.

"Eunice, who in their right mind would date that man? He lives with his mother and collects aspirin," Fran interjects.

"I'm sorry, he collects what?" I ask in bewilderment.

"Aspirin. Every size, shape, and color imaginable. He glues them to poster board and hangs them up all over his mother's house. I think he's a serial killer," Fran explains, dramatically whispering the last part.

"I think it's very artistic," my mother says indignantly. "I heard he even has aspirin from Germany."

"I'd be willing to bet next week's bingo winnings that those are roofies hanging all over his mother's house."

We all turn to stare at Fran.

"What are roofies? Are those the ones from Germany?" Eunice asks.

Fran opens her mouth to most likely school Eunice on all things roofies, and I quickly change the subject before this conversation goes downhill any faster.

"So, what do you guys think about Father Bob and the thefts that have been going on here?"

Fran huffs and lifts up her cane to point it at me. "It's just not right, Paige. What is this world coming to when a church isn't even safe? We should all get guns."

"Oh, my God, no! You should definitely not get any guns. That is a bad idea," I argue.

"Can I get a gun at Kroger? I have a coupon in my pocketbook for a dollar off any item," Eunice says excitedly.

"I say we handle this ourselves. Take back the church!" my mother shouts.

"TAKE BACK THE CHURCH!" Fran and Eunice echo.

I need to put a stop to this before it turns into all-out old-lady anarchy.

"No one is taking back anything! Mom, as soon as I get some free time this week, I will look into this, I promise."

Talk of guns is forgotten as Fran and Eunice begin discussing what dessert they'll be making for their Altar and Rosary meeting later this week.

"Don't you go to any trouble now, Paige. You just give Kennedy a call for me. I'm sure she'll be able to get to the bottom of it. In the meantime, I'll give Harold your number. Maybe he'll let you look at all his roofies."

CHAPTER 12

Grabbing three canisters of pepper spray from the junk drawer in my kitchen, I shove them into my bag. Slamming the drawer closed with my hip, I pause when I hear a knock at the door.

Maybe it's Lorelei. She knows I used her computer at the office to pull up old court records of Vinnie DeMarco so I could get his address. She knows I'm planning on staking out his house to see if Melanie shows up. If I'm real quiet, she'll go away. She won't break the door down like Kennedy if I don't answer.

"Paige, are you home? It's Matt."

The sound of his voice makes a lump form in my throat, especially since our last encounter wasn't a pleasant one.

On the way home from church with my mother the previous week, I stopped at the grocery store to pick up a few odds and ends. As I was walking back out to my car, my arms loaded with bags, I ran into Matt. Literally. I was losing the grip on one of the bags and as I stepped down off of the curb trying to juggle them, I barreled right into him. Of course the bag filled with all of the items a woman needs to get over a man spilled out at his feet: a family-size bag of Reese's Peanut Butter Cups, a gallon of Ben & Jerry's Chocolate

Fudge Brownie ice cream, two bottles of Hershey's Chocolate Syrup, a can of Reddi-wip, and a bottle of Moscato.

The universe hates me. I would have much preferred the bag of tampons and Midol had fallen at his feet.

I could do nothing but stare at him as he bent down to pick up everything I dropped. When he stood back up and wordlessly handed me the bag, he began to walk away without saying one word to me, and I finally shook myself out of the shock of seeing him again to speak.

"I swear I wasn't following you," I told him with a shaky laugh.

He didn't find it funny. He stuck his hands in his pockets and stared out at the parking lot. He couldn't even stand to look at me, and it made me want to sit down on the curb and immediately start making myself a Reese's Fudge Brownie Hershey Moscato sundae.

"Did you get my text?" I asked him lamely.

"Yep."

"Did you read it?" I tried again.

My heart thudded loudly in my ears. I knew this was my only chance to get him to understand and I was blowing it.

He sighed and turned back toward me, refusing to look at my face. His gaze landed somewhere between my chin and my neck. My plan of forcing him to look into my eyes and see that I was truly sorry wasn't going to work.

"Look, I have a lot going on in my life right now and I just don't have time for . . . this. Whatever this is. Or was. Fuck!" Matt cursed, his frustration with me evident.

"I'm so sorry, Matt," I whispered, willing the tears in my eyes not to fall and show him how much it hurts that he doesn't want anything to do with me.

"Yeah, well, I gotta go."

And with that, he brushed past me and into the grocery store.

———

I shake the depressing memory of our encounter last weekend out of my head and rush to the door. I probably shouldn't open it because he could very well be even angrier than Lorelei right now, but I want to see him. Even if it means I have to stand here and take it when he tells me how much he can't stand me.

"I didn't know if you'd answer," he says in greeting as I fling open the door.

Just like every time I see him, I'm taken aback by how good he looks. Even when he's frustrated or angry, I don't want to take my eyes off of him.

"What are you doing here? How did you know where I live?"

"I stopped by your office to cancel my request for a PI, and when your friend Lorelei went into the back to grab the file, I snooped through your desk and found some address labels," he tells me.

"Wow. That was pretty sneaky of you."

"Don't even start with me about being sneaky," Matt warns.

He softens the blow by smiling at me. I missed that smile. I'm such a sucker.

"Are you going somewhere?" he asks, pointing to the bag flung over my shoulder.

"First, tell me why you're here. If it's to inform me what a horrible person I am, I already got that memo last weekend."

He shoves his hands into the front pockets of his jeans and cocks his head. "You're not a horrible person. I'm sorry for losing my temper at the diner and for being so shitty at the store. It was just . . . a lot to take in and I was confused and hurt."

It takes everything in me not to reach out and touch him, not to wrap my arms around him and beg for his forgiveness. Even though I've been a sniveling mess since I screwed things up with him, and I miss him so much it hurts, I'm still me. Deep down I'm still the same strong, independent woman I found again after I left Andy, and I'm not about to put my heart on the line for someone until I know for sure the feelings are mutual. For all I know he just showed up here out of guilt for not giving me a chance to explain.

"I should have been honest with you. I just didn't expect everything to go down the way it did. That day you showed up at the office asking to hire us to trail Melanie, I freaked out."

Matt stares at me in confusion. "You were at the office that day?"

"Um, yeah. I was under Lorelei's desk," I admit sheepishly.

"So that's why she kept shifting in her chair and coughing. I thought something was seriously wrong with her," Matt says with a laugh. "Look, I've had some time to think about everything, and I get why you did what you did. Lorelei explained everything to me. Melanie hired you guys for some asinine reason and it was a conflict of interest for you to tell me anything when you met me. I should have never expected you to put your career or your friendships on the line for someone you just met."

I silently make a promise to myself to get Lorelei the best pair of shoes money can buy as a thank-you present for having my back even if she doesn't agree with what I've done.

Nodding my head, I move in closer to him in the doorway.

"I never meant to lie to you. Everything just snowballed so quickly. I wanted to tell you. As soon as you told me about her lawsuit and your father's company, I knew I had to help you."

Matt's face softens. "Why didn't you tell me about the whole modeling thing? I Googled you when I got home from the diner that night. Jesus Christ, Paige. You're like Cindy Crawford famous. You must have thought I was a total loser when I didn't know who you were."

I reach for Matt's hand, sliding my fingers through his.

"I never thought you were a loser, I swear. It's just, for practically my entire life, people have looked at me and immediately wondered how they could use my looks for their benefit. No one ever saw the real me or realized I might want something more out of my life than sitting in front of a camera. You saw the real me, and it was amazing to just be plain old Paige and not 'Paige McCarty, the model.' I probably could have gone about this whole mess a little better, but I honestly didn't know what to do without screwing over everyone I care about."

The corner of Matt's mouth tips up with a grin, and he takes another step closer to me until his chest is pressed right up against mine. "You make it so hard to stay mad at you. I have a thousand questions running through my head and all I can think about is kissing you again."

Smiling back at him, I place the palm of my hand over his heart and smile back. "Well, I think you should just—"

"Paige Elizabeth, stop canoodling in the doorway in front of God and everyone."

CHAPTER 13

I immediately pull back from Matt as my mother shoulders past us into my condo. "Do you have any Tums? My indigestion is flaring up."

Matt laughs behind me and my mother shoots him a dirty look. He immediately stops laughing and clears his throat.

"Who is this yahoo, and why is he standing in your doorway? Did you stand him up for one night—is that what this is?" she demands.

"It's 'one-night stand,' Mom, and no. This is my friend Matt. Matt, this is my mother, Margaret McCarty."

Matt moves around me and extends his hand out to her. "It's a pleasure to meet you, Mrs. McCarty."

My mother crosses her arms in front of her and glares at Matt. "It's Miss, not Mrs. Are you one of the people who takes indecent pictures of my daughter?"

Here we go again.

I sigh as Matt slowly brings his arm back down to his side when he sees my mother has no intention of shaking his hand. "No, Mom. He's not a photographer. And once again, they aren't indecent pictures."

"I saw your tush in the one you did for that *Maximum* magazine. Everyone in my needlepoint club saw your tush," she complains.

"It's called *Maxim*, Mom. And what were you doing reading *Maxim* magazine anyway?"

My mother shrugs and digs in her purse, finding a package of Kleenex and pulling one out. "I read it for the articles."

Matt chuckles while my mother blows her nose, her eyes zeroing in on the bag still draped over my shoulder.

"Are you going somewhere?" she asks, crumpling up the Kleenex and shoving it back into her purse.

"Actually, yes. I was just heading out to do some work when Matt showed up."

My mom purses her lips and crosses her arms over her chest again. "Are you doing nudie pictures again? No, don't tell me. I want to make sure I show enough shock on my face when Eunice and Fran tell me they saw your bump-bump at the supermarket checkout next to *Good Housekeeping*."

"Mom, I'm not doing nudie pictures or any pictures of any kind. I told you, I retired. I work full time at the private investigation firm," I remind her.

"I don't want to talk about your work as a prostitute."

Why do I bother . . .

"Uh, is there something else you want to tell me?" Matt whispers in my ear.

"I am not a prostitute!" I raise my voice to bring my point home.

"You kiss a bunch of men and get paid to do it," she reminds me.

"I'm an investigator, Mom. I'm paid to catch men who cheat on their wives."

My mother turns her angry glare to Matt and walks toward him. "Has my daughter kissed you?"

Matt's eyes widen in fear. He looks from my mother to me.

"Mom, cut it out."

"I'm going to take that as a 'yes,'" she tells Matt, completely ignoring my warning. "So you're a cheater. You don't look like a cheater. Andy looked like a cheater. I told Paige she should have never married that good-for-nothing."

"Matt is NOT a cheater, Mom. Matt is a good guy, so leave him alone. I really need to get going. I have work to do. Why don't I stop by next weekend for dinner?"

I slide my hand around her arm and gently steer her toward the door.

"I've got my bridge club next weekend, and Fran is making her Jell-O salad. I can't miss Fran's Jell-O salad. I'll just come with you to work."

I stop in my tracks and stare down at her. "You can't come to work with me. I'm going on a stakeout. It could be dangerous."

Yeah, not really. All I plan on doing is parking my car a block away from Vinnie DeMarco's house to see if Melanie makes an appearance. The most dangerous thing that will happen is not being able to say no to the ice cream truck when it drives by ten times.

My mother reaches her hand into her purse and this time, instead of a Kleenex, her hand comes back out with a revolver.

"JESUS CHRIST, MOM!"

"HOLY SHIT!"

Matt and I shout at the same time as we dive for the floor while she waves the gun around.

"Oh, for the love of Saint Patrick, will you get up off the ground? It's not even loaded. The bullets are in my glove box," Mom says with a roll of her eyes.

"What the hell are you doing with a gun?!" I screech at her from my position on the floor, flat on my stomach with my hands still covering my head.

"The church was broken into again two days ago during our Altar and Rosary meeting. They took the Communion hosts for the next few years this time," she explains. "We think it was Father John from Holy Cross because he plays poker every week with Father Bob, and Father Bob keeps winning. Father John is a sore loser. Anyway, it's a dangerous world out there when someone starts stealing Communion. Eunice and I went up to the gun shop and got ourselves some protection. Get up off the floor. I can't talk to you down there."

I stare up at her as she points the gun at me while she speaks.

"Could you please aim the gun elsewhere?" I mutter.

My mother sighs in irritation and lowers her arm. Matt pushes himself up off the floor when he sees it's safe to do so, reaches down, and pulls me up next to him. "What exactly is this stakeout you speak of?"

Brushing myself off, I stare at Matt's ass as he turns away from me, bends over, and picks up my bag that fell to the ground during my dive to safety.

He really has a great ass.

My eyes flick away guiltily as he turns around and smirks at me.

"I found out where Vinnie DeMarco lives. I'm going to park down the street and see if Melanie shows up."

Matt stares at me in shock. "Wait, you've still been working on this even after everything that happened?"

I shrug. "Well, yeah. It's not fair, what she's doing to you. I couldn't just let that go."

He has a really good poker face right now and doesn't give away anything that he's thinking. I hope this goes a little way toward proving to him that he can trust me.

"I'm coming with you."

It's not even a question. He just tells me what he's going to do. With my sense of independence since I kicked Andy's ass to the curb, I don't take too kindly to people telling me what to do. Matt leans in close to me and brushes a lock of hair off of my cheek. "If that's okay with you."

Son of a bitch.

A gun with an arm attached to it suddenly shoves its way between our bodies. "Save room for the Holy Ghost. Let's get a move on. I need to get some food in my stomach so I can take my arthritis medication."

My mom pushes her way between the two of us and walks out into the sunshine.

I grudgingly follow behind her, leading the way for Matt to follow. I close and lock the door behind us and slide my hand into his as we walk down the front steps toward the parking lot, where my mother is already tapping her foot next to the passenger-side door.

I can't help being a little embarrassed. This whole thing with Matt didn't exactly start off under great circumstances, and now I'm dragging him out for an afternoon with my insane mother. Even if I did still believe in fairy tales and happily ever after, I'd have to light that romantic notion on fire at this point. I'm a little shocked he didn't crash through the front door like a cartoon character as soon as she pulled her gun from her bag.

"If this is too weird for you, you don't have to come with us," I tell him, stopping far enough away from my car so my mother doesn't hear us.

"I'm not going to lie—this is all a little crazy right now. I like you. A lot. And that scares the shit out of me because I don't know if I can trust you. You're going out on a limb to help me and I don't know if it's because you have feelings for me or you just feel guilty."

When I open my mouth to tell him it has absolutely nothing to do with guilt and everything to do with how I feel about him, he holds a hand up to stop me.

"Don't. Just . . . not yet. I'm not trying to be mean or ungrateful for what you're doing. I just need time for my brain to process everything," he admits.

I put on my big-girl panties and nod at him, not letting his words cut a hole in my heart. I know what he's going through. I know what it's like to lose your trust in someone and struggle to find it again. I just never thought I would be the one someone didn't trust. At least he still thinks about kissing me, so there's that.

"Well, a stakeout in my VW Bug with my seventy-year-old, gun-toting, arthritic mother sounds like a great way for you to start processing things, doesn't it?" I ask dryly.

"As long as you don't leave me alone with Margaret and her gun, I think this will be a good start." Matt smiles at me as I hit the button on my key chain to unlock the doors to my car.

CHAPTER 14

"A m I the first person ever to stare at you blankly when you told me your name? You must have thought I was an idiot."

Leaning my head back against the seat, I stare over at Matt. He mirrors my pose and I scoot my body a little closer to him.

"I told you, I'm not offended, believe me. I was serious when I said I liked it that you didn't know who I was. It was nice being able to talk to someone who didn't know anything about me," I admit to him.

Matt slides over to the edge of his seat as well until there are only a few inches and a gearshift separating us. "I really can't thank you enough that you're doing this for me. Are your friends going to hate you when they find out what happened?"

The concern in his voice melts my heart. He's about to lose the company his father worked hard for all his life, his ex is dating a mobster who might fit us for cement shoes if he finds us trailing him, and he's worried about my well-being.

Where did this guy come from?

"Lorelei already knows, sort of. She hasn't told Kennedy yet, and that's a little concerning. Kennedy is the one we need to worry about. She carries a gun," I tell him with a smile. "But seriously, once we get this all figured out and I can explain to her what happened, she's going to understand. I know it."

Matt leans across the gearshift, meeting me in the middle until I can feel his breath on my face. "But this is the Mob we're dealing with. I don't want anything to happen to you because of me."

I've never wanted to kiss someone so badly in my entire life. I still remember how soft his lips were and how he tasted. I remember the feel of his tongue sliding against mine and how tightly his arms wrapped around my body, holding me close to him. Memories aren't doing it for me right now, though. I need the real thing.

Staring into his gorgeous eyes, I start to close the distance between us, the sound of my heartbeat thumping in my ears with excitement.

"How long are we going to just sit here? My bursitis is acting up."

With a sigh, I pull away from Matt and glare at my mother as she opens the rear door and gets back in from stretching her legs. I guess that wasn't my heart I heard pounding a few moments ago. It was her stomping her foot against the ground trying to get some feeling back in her legs.

"I didn't ask you to come with us. You could have stayed at my place," I remind her.

"I thought this stakeout thing would be a little more exciting."

Turning away from her, I give Matt an apologetic look and he smiles back at me. Even with my mother complaining in the backseat, I still can't stop thinking about kissing him again. Or imagining him naked. Is it wrong that my mother is two feet away and I'm wondering what it would feel like to run my hands all over his naked body? Matt's eyes darken as he stares back at me, almost like he knows what I'm thinking.

"So that's what a shameful walk looks like. I've always wondered."

Breaking from my lustful thoughts, I look back at my mother and see her staring out her window. Whipping my head around, I see Melanie coming down the front steps of Vinnie DeMarco's home. She's carrying a pair of heels in her hand, she's got mascara smudged under her eyes, and her hair looks like a rat's nest.

"It's 'walk of shame,' Mom," I mutter as all three of us stare silently at Melanie while she stands at the end of the driveway, looking up and down the street.

A few minutes later, a taxi pulls up and she hops into the backseat. Matt and I duck down at the same time as the taxi slowly drives past my car.

"The coast is clear," my mother informs us.

As I sit up I look over at Matt to see how he's doing. "Are you okay?"

He rights himself in his seat and stares straight out the front window to the end of Vinnie's driveway, which Melanie just vacated.

Shit. Why in the hell do I do this to myself? I shouldn't be lusting after someone who's still hung up on his ex.

He just witnessed her leaving another man's home. I mean, he had a feeling she was seeing someone else, but now he pretty much has proof since she just left the guy's house with her hair looking like it spent plenty of hours on another man's pillow.

"Matt?" I whisper his name and he finally blinks out of his daze and looks over at me. When he sees the worry on my face, he smiles reassuringly at me.

"It's just weird. I mean, I've known her since college. At one time she was my best friend. I knew this was happening, but it's just . . . I don't know. Hard to see it with my own eyes."

I swallow roughly and try not to let it bother me that he's hurt over that lying skank.

I remove my hand from its death grip on the steering wheel. I slide my fingers through his and give his hand a gentle squeeze.

"I didn't even get to use my gun." Mom sniffs irritably from the backseat, and just like that, I stop feeling sorry for myself. "Can we get some food now? I need to take my pills."

—◆—

After stopping at a diner on our way home, my mom hops out of my car as soon as I pull into my parking spot, telling me to keep her posted and that if I need her help, to give her a call.

Matt and I stand silently next to my car, and watch her pull out of the parking lot and drive away.

"Well, that was informative," Matt says with a laugh.

"Sorry about all of those childhood stories she bored you with. I swear I don't make up dances to Madonna songs anymore and force my mother and her friends to watch me perform them over dinner."

Matt moves in front of me and brushes a strand of hair out of my eyes with his fingertips.

"I don't know; I think I'd kind of like to see you shaking your thing to 'Like a Virgin,'" he laughs.

I smack him playfully in the chest, leaving my hand to rest over his heart. When I feel the muscles of his pecs under my hands, my brain immediately goes right into lusty territory, and I wonder again what he looks like naked. And how soon I can get a glimpse of said nakedness.

We stare silently at each other for several minutes. The butterflies in my stomach are threatening to escape if he doesn't do something soon. Something like kiss the ever-living hell out of me.

I know I should back away. I can tell he's trying to forget about what he saw earlier and there's an internal war going on inside of him right now. Before I can move away from him, he shakes his head and curses.

"Fuck it."

He grabs my face in his hands and pulls me to him. As soon as our lips touch, I know I'm never going to pass up a chance to kiss this man. Matt doesn't waste any time deepening the kiss and I moan into his mouth when his tongue skims against mine. Bringing my arms up to his shoulders, I pull him closer. He leans his body against mine, pressing me against the side of my car.

This man knows how to kiss. His lips are soft, yet firm, and his tongue does delicious things to me as it swirls though my mouth. Desire pools in my stomach and my hips instinctively shift against him. I want to feel him everywhere. I want his hands on my naked body and I want him inside me. I've never craved anyone this much, not even Andy. I was attracted to him, and sex with him was always good, but I never felt like I would die if I didn't have him.

Matt's hands drop from my face and slide around my hips to cup my ass, pulling me harder against him. I can feel the evidence of his need for me and it just makes everything sweeter. Every slide of his tongue, every press of his lips, every whisper of air he breathes into me is so delectable that I never want it to end.

He gently sucks my tongue into his mouth and thrusts his hips between my legs. I can feel his erection sliding against me and my need for him climbs to new heights. I can't stop myself from pushing back against him, the desire I feel taking over where common sense left off. We're dry humping each other against the side of my car in broad daylight, and his kiss made me completely forget that just an hour ago, he was saddened by the sight of seeing his ex leaving another man's house.

A car honks in the distance, and Matt pulls his mouth away from mine. "I really, really need to leave," he tells me softly, pressing his forehead against mine.

"Oh, okay." I can't keep the dejection out of my voice.

I really don't understand why he can't just bang me on the hood of the car.

Oh, that's right, because I'm better than this and I need him to want me for me and not just as a distraction.

"I don't want to go, I swear. But if I don't leave right now, I'm going to take you upstairs, lock the door, and refuse to come out until we're both naked, sweaty, and exhausted."

I'm sorry, what's the problem again?

I nod my head like I completely understand what he's talking about. Why can't he just forget about Melanie already?

"I know as soon as I walk away from you I'm going to regret saying this, but I just think we need to take this slow. I've already got one fucked-up relationship under my belt. I want things to be different this time."

I can't fault him for his honesty. I need to prove to him that he can trust me, and I suppose slow and truthful is better than hurried and naked. For now.

"It's okay, I get it. But just know, when we finally are naked and sweaty, I'll make sure you won't have anything on your mind except for what I'm doing to you," I tell him with a wink.

He groans, and by the look on his face, I'm pretty sure he's second-guessing his noble efforts. I laugh and kiss him quickly on the lips and then move back before I take him against his will on the sidewalk. While fun, I don't think the neighbors would appreciate the show.

I make sure to add a little extra sway to my hips as I walk away from him. Just because we're taking things slow doesn't mean I can't torture him just a little.

"You're killing me, Paige McCarty!" Matt shouts to me as I climb up the stairs and put my key in the lock.

I can't keep the smile off of my face as I open the door and leave him outside on the sidewalk to think about what he's missing. I hear his truck start up and pull away a few seconds later as I flop down on the couch, tossing my bag onto the coffee table. Seeing a piece of paper sitting on the glass top, I lean forward and pick it up. The smile dies on my face when I see the words scribbled across it in perfectly neat, block letters:

IF YOU KNOW WHAT'S GOOD FOR YA, YOU'LL STOP STICKIN YOUR NOSE WHERE IT DON'T BELONG. GO BACK TO BEING IN PRETTY PICTURES AND NO ONE GETS HURT.

I drop the note like it's on fire and scramble up from the couch, staring frantically around my condo, afraid to breathe.

Someone was in my home. Someone knows I've been looking into Vinnie DeMarco. What if they're still here?

For the first time today, I wish my mother were here with her gun.

CHAPTER 15

W̲e're going to the fucking police right now," Matt states angrily as he hits the blinker in his F-150 truck to take us into town.

When I ran out of my house in a panic, I pulled my phone out of my purse and called the first person I thought of. Was it just because I could still taste him on my lips? I could have called my mom, but I knew she would just lecture me, and I could have called Kennedy, but that would mean I'd have to come clean about what I'd been doing and I wasn't ready for that. The only person I wanted in the midst of my fear was Matt. It exhilarated me and scared the shit out of me all at the same time.

I'd grown used to my independence in the months since my divorce, and it was a frightening feeling to want to depend on another person again. Especially one of the male gender who could fuck me over in the blink of an eye and crush my heart to pieces if he suddenly decided he was still in love with his lying, cheating ex.

"There's no need to get the police involved. I probably over-reacted. For all I know it was Andy trying to cause trouble because I won't give him any money."

He stops at the empty intersection and stares across the front seat of the truck at me. I can see the battle going on in his eyes. He wants so much to protect me from the person who left a threatening note in my house, but he also wants to do whatever I ask.

"I don't like this, Paige. I don't like this at all."

Then he sighs deeply and takes the street that leads away from downtown and away from the police.

Andy would always make decisions for me. He would tell me that he was doing what he thought was in my best interest or say that the few years in age he had on me meant that he was able to make more informed choices about my life. Really, he wanted to make me feel like I needed him to function. For the first few months after we separated, I almost believed it. I didn't know how to do anything on my own. I didn't remember how to make the simplest of decisions because I had been relying on him for so long. With the help of my friends, I was able to see just how much he controlled my life and slowly get my independence back.

Something as little as having Matt listen to me when I tell him what I want means more to me than he'll ever know. He didn't belittle me or tell me that I didn't know what I was talking about. He let me make my own decision, even if it turns out to be the wrong one.

I feel my throat growing tight with unshed tears and I have to clear it to keep them at bay. I will not cry right now.

"I wish you would have let me look through your place. What if whoever left that note was still there?" Matt asks.

"Are you crazy? That's like something straight out of a horror movie. You never go back into a house looking for the bad people. It always ends with a machete to the face," I argue.

"A machete, huh? Do you normally have a lot of people with machetes after you?" Matt asks with a laugh. "I'm seriously considering turning the truck around and going back to the police if that's the case."

"Like I said, I probably just made a big deal out of nothing. I'll get hold of Andy first thing tomorrow and put the fear of God into him."

"And if it wasn't that little weasel, what then? Your friends aren't sick and twisted enough to do this as some sort of joke, are they?" he asks.

I'm not going to lie; it warms my heart even more that he called Andy a weasel.

I laugh easily at the idea that Kennedy and Lorelei would sneak into my house and leave a note like that for me, the heaviness of my thoughts from a moment ago disappearing quickly. "Okay, I think it's safe to say Lorelei would have never done something like that. She would have used bigger words to drive her point home, and she would have been more polite. Like, 'Please discontinue your inquisitive ways or we shall be obliged to damage your appendages,'" I tell him in my best Lorelei voice.

"I would have to agree even though I've only talked to her for a few minutes. But what about Kennedy? She carries a gun and she sounds scary," Matt says with a dramatic shiver. The smile on his face proves that he believed me when I said they wouldn't do something like this, and he's trying to distract me by making light of the situation.

"Well, it's close to something Kennedy would have said, but hers would have had more cursing. 'Get your fucking head out of your ass before I punch you in the goddamn face.'"

Matt and I laugh together as I describe my friend's personalities to him with just a few sentences.

"I'm glad you called me," he says softly as he pulls into a driveway of a gorgeous Cape Cod home and puts his truck in park.

He doesn't give me a chance to reply as he jumps out of the truck and comes around to my side, opening the door for me and taking my hand to help me down. Hand in hand we walk up the steps of his front porch, and I stand to the side, admiring his profile as he unlocks the front door.

As soon as we walk inside, Matt hits a switch and bathes the living room in light. I have to say, I'm a little shocked at what I see. I assumed his place would look similar to Andy's apartment: mismatched furniture, no pictures on the wall, still-unpacked boxes littering the floors, and takeout containers in the kitchen. Matt's home is tastefully decorated and spotless. There aren't any signs that a woman used to live here, but it also doesn't look like a bachelor pad. It's gray and black and full of leather, and I love it. I notice a framed picture on an end table next to the couch, and I walk right up to it and lift it up for a better look. In the picture, Matt has his arm around the shoulders of an older man; it almost looks like a before-and-after picture. I can tell right away that this is Matt's father and also how nicely Matt is going to age. His father is a handsome man with the same bright blue eyes and dark hair as his son, except he has a few gray hairs at his temples and wrinkles around his eyes.

"This is a great picture. I'm assuming this is your dad?"

Matt comes up behind me and looks over my shoulder. "Yep. That's Eric Russo. Obviously, he gets his good looks from me."

I laugh, setting the picture back down and turning around to face him.

"Can you show me where the bathroom is? I want to wash up a little. And if you have anything I can use as pajamas, that would be good too. I didn't think to grab anything when I went racing out of my house like a chicken."

Matt places his hands on my shoulders, sliding them up my neck until he cups my cheeks. "I'm sure I can find something for you to wear. And you aren't a chicken. I would have gone screaming into the night if someone left a note like that for me too."

My heart skips a beat as he places a kiss on the tip of my nose before grabbing my hand and pulling me down the hallway.

I can't keep the smile off of my face as I stare at myself in the mirror. I washed off the day's makeup and ran a comb through my hair. I'm wearing an old T-shirt of Matt's and a pair of his boxer shorts and I've never felt more comfortable. As I head for the door, I pull the neck of the shirt up to my nose and take a deep breath, loving how it smells exactly like Matt.

I step out of the bathroom and into the hall, walking over to Matt's room to thank him and say good-night. Instead of letting things turn awkward when it came time to discuss sleeping arrangements, as soon as he handed me the T-shirt and boxers, I told him I was fine sleeping on the couch. He tried to argue with me and give me his bed, but I wouldn't have it. He's done enough for me tonight; I'm not about to make him give up his bed. Or beg him to let me sleep in it with him.

I poke my head into his bedroom and lose my breath when I see him resting on top of his covers. He's shirtless and has on a pair of gray sweatpants, and his hands are resting under his head with his feet crossed at the ankles. His eyes slowly open as I hover in the doorway.

He takes me in from head to toe and I feel a little self-conscious when I remember I'm not wearing a stitch of makeup.

"You are so beautiful," Matt says in awe.

I can't even tell you how many times I've heard this back in my modeling days. But hearing it come out of a man's mouth when I'm fresh faced and wearing one of his shirts and a pair of his boxers, it warms every single spot inside of me.

"Why are you still standing all the way over there? Come here."

He slides over and pats the bed next to him. I should turn and run down the stairs—I really should.

"I don't know if that's a good idea," I hedge as I stare at the happy trail disappearing into the waistband of his pajama pants.

"It's an excellent idea. Just let me hold you for a little while."

His voice is soft and no longer teasing. I can see in his face that he's concerned about me. Even though we made jokes and I tried to convince myself that Andy was the one who left me that creepy note, we both know there is a strong possibility someone much more dangerous could be out there watching me. In the dim light of his quiet bedroom this late at night, I realize Matt would never judge me for being weak, or admitting I'm scared and don't want to be alone right now.

Padding across the floor in my bare feet, I crawl up the bed until I'm next to him, curling up against his side and resting my cheek on his chest. I trace little circles on his stomach with my fingertips and watch as his stomach dips when I ghost over a ticklish spot.

"Thank you for coming to my rescue tonight," I whisper against his skin.

Matt's hand threads its way through the long strands of my hair over and over. "I'm glad you called me. I like having you here, wearing my clothes."

I can hear the smile in his voice and I lift my head so I can see his face. He stares down at me with one arm still resting casually under his head. Lifting my face up to his, I press my lips against his cheek and hold them there. When I pull away, Matt is staring into my eyes. All worries about threatening notes and him being in love with Melanie fly from my mind, and all I can think about is getting closer to him. Grabbing onto my hips, he pulls me on top of him. With my legs straddling him and my chest pressed against his, I feel every hard inch of him between my legs; nothing separates us but a few scraps of cotton. Leaning up, I reach for the hem of Matt's shirt that covers my body and pull it over my head. He sucks in a breath when I'm bared to him and his hands immediately come up to cover my breasts.

"I know I talked a good game earlier about taking things slow. Obviously that's not going to work out for me. If you're not sure, or if this is too fast, we don't have to do this," he whispers softly as he stares at his hands moving gently over my breasts, his thumbs sliding over my nipples and causing me to jerk my hips against him.

"Not fast enough. Definitely not fast enough."

Resting my hands on top of his, I lean back down and kiss him. He lifts his hips against me with each sweep of his tongue through my mouth and I want more. I can't get close enough, can't move my body fast enough against him. We quickly pull away from each other and clothes are ripped off and tossed to the side of the bed. I let out a contented sigh when we're both naked, skin to skin, hands touching everywhere we can reach. Matt lets out a groan when my hand wraps around his length and I stroke him from top to bottom. He's smooth and hard in my hand. I could spend the entire night touching him.

"Fuck, Paige. I need you."

The guttural words from Matt's mouth turn me on more than I thought possible.

"Then hurry your ass up and take me."

I let out a squeak of surprise when Matt suddenly flips me onto my back and positions himself between my legs. He slides his erection through my wetness until I'm clutching at his back with my nails, trying to pull him closer. The head of his penis moves back and forth over my clit and I feel that familiar coil deep in my belly, signaling my quickly approaching orgasm. I watch between our bodies as Matt grabs his erection and guides it slowly inside of me. Throwing my head back, I moan when I feel him enter me and push his way inside. He's thick and hard and nothing has ever felt this amazing or this right.

He pulls back out slowly and my hands grab onto his ass, pulling him back in hard. He starts up a delicious rhythm with his hips, not treating me like a delicate flower, and then thrusts into me over and over and my hips push up against him, trying to force him harder and deeper. Wrapping my legs around his waist I let him take me, claim me, and own me. My orgasm bursts out of me, and Matt swallows my cries with his mouth. I kiss him back hard, moving my hands up to the back of his head and holding him in place while he shudders and groans through his own release a few minutes later. I feel him throbbing inside of me and tighten my legs around him, holding him close.

Through the haze of my orgasm and the distraction of Matt's tongue lazily stroking through my mouth, I hear the ringing of my cell phone on Matt's bedside table. Moving my head away from him, I crane my head to check the caller ID while he nestles his face into the side of my neck and places soft kisses against my skin.

"Just let it ring." Matt speaks against my neck.

"I have no intention of answering it, don't worry," I reassure him as I run my fingers through his hair.

When I see the name flash across my screen, I can't help the surprised word that flies from my mouth. "Andy?"

Matt's head jerks away from my neck and he stares down at me.

"Did you just say your ex-husband's name while my penis is still inside of you?"

Looking away from my phone, I see the irritated look in Matt's face and I instantly feel bad.

"I'm sorry! This is a little awkward. I saw his name on my caller ID. I have no idea why he's calling me."

Matt reaches over and grabs my phone, bringing it up to his

ear without taking his eyes off of me. "Sorry, Andy. Paige is busy right now; she'll have to call you later. And by later, I mean never."

He quickly ends the call and tosses the phone onto the floor. "I hope that was okay. I don't need your ex-husband in the room with us. I'm not quite finished with you yet."

He shifts his hips against me and I let out a moan. "That is perfectly fine with me."

CHAPTER 16

Paige? Oh, my God, Oh, my God, Oh, my God. Who the hell was that who answered your phone? Fuck, it doesn't matter. It's really bad. Those people I told you I owe money to . . . they grabbed me outside of work. They're going to kill me, Paige! They want their money by the weekend, or they said they're going to start cutting off my fingers. MY FINGERS, Paige! I need my fingers! They want a hundred grand now. I need you to—"

Holding my phone out in front of me with a shaking hand, I look up when the voice mail cuts off. Dallas Osborne, a friend and private investigator with a neighboring PI agency, stands quietly by my desk with his hands on his hips. His face gives nothing away. I called Dallas as soon as I listened to the voice mail, and he said he'd meet me at the office so I could play him the message. He's listened to it three times now, and each time, he's said nothing other than a quiet "play it again." Lorelei stands next to him, wringing her hands together with a look of worry on her face. I didn't want to involve my friends in this, but Lorelei was at the office finishing up some work when we all showed up. She hasn't said a word yet, and I'm afraid of what will happen when she finally does open her mouth. She is not going to be happy with me that I've let things go this far without telling Kennedy.

I've already listened to this voice mail a hundred times since Matt and I woke up this morning, and I'm freaking out enough as it is. I don't know if I can handle Lorelei's wrath as well. As much as I hate Andy, I would never want to see him dead. It's all fun and games to imagine lighting your ex's penis on fire until you get a call from him in the middle of the night saying someone is going to kill him.

"What do we do, Dallas?" I ask as I set my phone on top of my desk.

"We need to call Kennedy. That's what we need to do," Lorelei states.

"I already called Kennedy. She's in Indianapolis with Griffin serving a subpoena. I figured it was best not to worry her," Dallas explains.

"Are you kidding me right now? She SHOULD be worried. I knew I should have told her what you were up to weeks ago."

"Oh, pipe down, lawyer. I've got this under control."

Lorelei puts her hands on her hips and stares angrily at Dallas. "Who the hell do you think you are? You don't even work here."

Dallas crosses his arms over his chest and stares her down. "I'm the guy who's going to get you out of this mess. Don't you have a case to try or something? Go away."

Lorelei huffs indignantly, and if she wasn't such a lady, I'm sure a whole bunch of profanities would be flying from her mouth right now. For some reason, Lorelei and Dallas have never gotten along. He thinks she's too uptight, and she thinks he's a Neanderthal.

"You are a pompous jerk!" Lorelei shouts.

"Really? That's the best you can do? Are all your clients on death row now?" Dallas taunts.

"Can we please get back to the problem at hand?" I interrupt. "What are we going to do about Andy?"

Dallas looks at Lorelei smugly one last time before turning his focus to me. "We wait for Andy to call back with the drop-off location. In the meantime, you need to figure out a way to get a hundred thousand dollars by the weekend."

"You can't be serious," Lorelei says. "We need to call the police."

"Woman, I've already talked to the police, so don't get your panties all in a bunch," Dallas replies with a roll of his eyes.

"You did NOT just call me 'woman'!"

Ignoring the fight in front of me, I turn to look at Matt and see the worry written all over his face.

"I'll give you the hundred grand," Matt tells me.

I shake my head at him and put my foot down. "You are not going to help me with this. He's my ex and I'll deal with it. I'm not some poor, defenseless female who constantly needs rescuing, contrary to my actions last night."

Matt puts his hands on either side of my face and forces me to look up at him. "Don't do that. Don't lump me into the same category as Andy. I have never treated you like you were defenseless or weak. You are one of the strongest women I've ever met. I care about you, Paige. And I'm just worried about you. I don't want anything happening to you."

Bringing my hands up to rest on top of his against my cheeks, I sigh and smile at him.

"I'm a private investigator, Matt. I may not have a lot of experience in the field, but this is what I do. If I want people to take me seriously as a PI, then I need to be able to handle my personal life on my own. I am not going to let you bail my ex-husband out of the mess he got himself into. It's not your problem."

"It's not your problem either, Paige," he tells me softly.

"But I'm going to take care of it anyway, on my own."

More shouting interrupts our moment.

"Stop being such an egotistical brute!"

"At least I'm not an uptight bitch!" Dallas yells back to her.

"You two need to just have sex already," I mutter with a shake of my head.

⌒

I can't believe I'm doing this again. I swore I was done with this business when I left Andy, and yet, here I am, sitting in a chair getting poked and prodded with curling irons, mascara wands, and tubes of lipstick. Five minutes back in this business and I already feel only good for one thing.

My agent, Penny, comes bustling up to me with a huge grin on her face.

"Darling, it's so good to see you back doing what you do best. Didn't I tell you that police-officer thing was silly?"

Moving away from the makeup artist with a brush aimed at my eye, I turn to look at Penny. "I'm not working as a police officer. I told you, it's a private investigation business."

Penny laughs and checks her reflection in the mirror in front of me, fluffing up her hair and wiping a smudge of lipstick off of her teeth.

"Same thing. Stick with what you're good at, darling. You'll only have your looks for so long."

Satisfied with her reflection, Penny pats me on the shoulder and walks away to shout orders at the photographer and his assistants.

"Can I have a few minutes, please?" I ask the makeup artist, whose name I didn't get.

"I'm finished. Just don't get your face wet or go outside. It's windy, and it will take me forever to get those curls just right again."

She walks away quickly in a huff. It's always the same thing at these photo shoots. Everyone treats me like I'm an idiot.

"Wow, you look—"

"Don't say it. Please don't say it," I warn Matt as he comes up behind me and stares at my reflection.

I really don't need to hear him tell me how beautiful and amazing I look. It's not really me. It's just makeup and hairspray. And besides, they're going to Photoshop the heck out of me anyway.

But this is who I used to be and he needs to get a glimpse of that.

Even though I said I was going to do this on my own, I wanted Matt to be here with me. If he's going to trust me, he needs to see all of me—the good, the bad, and the modeling. In the midst of all the craziness going on with his life—meeting with lawyers and talking to his board of directors to get all of their ducks in a row before they have to go to court against Melanie—he took the time out of his busy schedule to show up for this shoot. If I didn't know it already, this would just solidify the fact that I'm falling hard for him.

"I was going to tell you that you look like the Bride of Frankenstein with all that crap on your face. I think a few pictures of you just wearing one of my T-shirts would be much better."

I feel tears well up in my eyes and I blink quickly to keep them contained, but it's no use. A few slide down my face and I swipe them away before anyone notices I messed up my makeup.

"Oh, great. Now I'm going to have to fix her foundation. Who made her cry?!" I hear the makeup artist shout from somewhere behind us but I don't care. Matt just said the most wonderful words to me ever.

I stare at him through the mirror while my foundation is reapplied. He walks up closer and rests his hands on my shoulders. "I'm sorry. I should know better than to insult a beautiful woman."

I laugh and shake my head at him. "Believe me, that wasn't an insult. That was beautiful."

The makeup artist touches up my face, shooting Matt dirty looks the entire time.

"I can't believe this is what your life was like for so many years. People dressing you and fussing over you. Did you see the craft service table over there? There's lobster on it, Paige. Lobster," he stresses with a smile.

"I know. It's hard to believe I gave all of this up for the glamorous life of catching bad guys. I'm lucky if Kennedy brings in bagels once a month."

When the makeup artist is satisfied with her touch-up, she walks away and leaves us alone again.

"I'm glad you asked me to come. Even though the food table is a thing of beauty, I think I understand. This isn't you, Paige," he tells me, gesturing at all the people rushing around setting things up for the shoot. "You shouldn't just sit in front of a camera and not have a say in what happens. You're smart and you're strong and you should be doing something that makes you happy. Watching you take charge and do what you were trained to do at Fool Me Once—that's you. That's who you were meant to be."

It's amazing that this man who has only known me for a handful of weeks gets it. He can see the mold I've been trying to break out of.

"Thank you, Matt. You have no idea how much that means to me. I'm glad you're here," I tell him softly.

Matt looks at me sheepishly. "You might want to take that back when you see who I brought with me. The board meeting ran a little late today, and my dad's car is in the shop, so I had to give him a ride home."

"Is it too hard to get a chair in this godforsaken place? I got bad hips."

Looking over Matt's shoulder, I see the man who was in the photograph with Matt at his house. Except he's not smiling and looks a little irritated as he walks up to us.

"Matthew, that man over there has an earring in his nose. Is he a gay?"

Matt closes his eyes and shakes his head. "Dad, I told you to stay in the car."

His father grunts and walks over to my chair in front of the mirror, taking a seat and crossing his arms in front of him. "I couldn't figure out that fancy radio of yours."

Matt walks to my side and puts his arm around my waist. "Dad, this is Paige McCarty. Paige, this is my father, Eric Russo."

I reach my hand out to him with a smile. "It's nice to meet you, Mr. Russo."

He just stares at me and after a few seconds, I drop my hand back to my side.

"Are you going to be taking your clothes off for these pictures, young lady?" Mr. Russo asks.

"DAD!" Matt scolds.

A laugh bubbles out of me. "It's okay, Matt. No, Mr. Russo, I will not be taking my clothes off for this photo shoot. This is for a well-known magazine, so clothing is required."

Mr. Russo narrows his eyes at me. "It's a good thing I came in here. I see a lot of charlatans in this room who could lead you astray. Like that woman over there with the blue hair and pink skirt."

I turn around and see that he's staring right at the photographer for this shoot.

"Actually, that's a man. His name is Simon Viper, and he's one of the best photographers in the world," I tell him.

Mr. Russo's eyes go wide. "This world is going to hell in a handbasket. Matt, get me some ginger ale. I'm feeling parched."

Matt sighs and gives me an apologetic look as the photographer's assistant signals to me that it's time to start the shoot. I kiss Matt on the cheek and hear Mr. Russo mumble as I walk away.

"If she takes her clothes off, you better cover your eyes, Matthew."

I just laugh, unable to believe there is someone else in this world who reminds me so much of my mother. The two of them should meet and share notes about what a sinner I am.

CHAPTER 17

For the first time in a long while during a photo shoot, I actually enjoyed myself. Anytime I felt a twinge of irritation, all I had to do was look over at Matt. The shouts and orders telling me which way to turn my head and how to hold my arms faded before the warmth in his smile.

When the final shot was taken and the photographer announced it was a wrap, I walked away from the bright lights and the fans strategically placed to blow my hair, and slid right into Matt's waiting arms.

"You did amazing. I saw some of the pictures as they showed up on the computer and they were beautiful."

What a difference a year makes. Last year at this time, I would finish a photo shoot and Andy would tell me all the ways I could have done better. He would walk me over to the computer that showed all of the digital images and point out the ones where my face didn't hit the light correctly or I wasn't using my angles in the best way.

"Great job today, Paige," Simon says as he walks up to us, handing his camera off to an assistant. "We'll send the proofs to Penny within a week so you can see them first before they go to print. We got some great shots to work with."

With my arms still around Matt, I thank Simon as he's hustled away by an army of assistants and Penny comes over to us.

"Darling, you were amazing. The magazine gave me your advance: fifty percent of the total offer; you'll get the rest when the photos go to print. I'll deposit it today for you."

She pulls the check for seventy-five thousand dollars out of her purse and I quickly snatch it from her hand. It's not the entire amount DeMarco is asking for, but it will have to do. "No need to go to all that trouble. I'll take care of it."

Penny gives me a strange look and I don't blame her. I've never taken care of anything in my career. Andy made sure I had people who did that for me. But I'm pretty sure whoever has Andy isn't going to want to wait for this check to clear before they get their money.

"I've got a bunch more jobs lined up for you, so make sure to keep your schedule open. I'm so glad you're back," Penny tells me.

"Penny, I'm not back. This was a onetime thing. I have another job now."

Seriously, how many times do we have to go over this?

"Oh, sweetie, you were blessed with a gorgeous face and an equally stunning body. Let's not fool ourselves into believing you'll be successful at anything else. I would hate to see you sad when it all comes crashing down. This is what you are meant to do."

I feel the familiar ache of despair in the pit of my stomach at her words. This woman, who has been by my side for more than ten years, thinks I'm only good for one thing. Before I can tell her where she can shove her opinions, Matt takes a step forward.

"I think it would be in your best interest to stop talking and walk away," Matt tells Penny with a scowl on his face.

Penny looks up at him in shock. "I'm just being honest."

"No, what you're doing is being a bitch. This woman right here is amazing, and she can do whatever she puts her mind to. The last person who put her down like that received a punch to the face, so you might want to quit while you're ahead."

I can't stop the smile from spreading across my face. Penny quietly apologizes to me and scurries away without another word.

"I don't know whether to be flattered or horrified that you would punch a woman for me."

Matt shrugs. "I would never hit a woman. But it was fun making her think that I would. I know you can take care of yourself, and you probably would have done a better job telling that woman off, but I couldn't let her talk to you like that."

Suddenly, nothing else matters right now but getting this man naked. Immediately.

Grabbing his hand, I pull him out of the studio and down the hall. "Where's your dad?"

"He asked one of the assistants to pray with him. When she told him she didn't believe in God, he threw his ginger ale at her. I sent him back out to the truck with firm instructions not to leave unless it caught on fire."

Pulling open the first door I come to, I flip the switch right inside and see that it's a supply closet filled with camera equipment. Glancing around to make sure no one sees us, I pull Matt inside and close the door behind us.

"What are we doing in here?" Matt asks.

His eyes go wide as I pull the zipper down on the side of my dress and let it fall from my shoulders. I'm standing in front of him in nothing but a black lace thong and four-inch black stilettos.

"Take your pants off," I order him.

Matt doesn't waste a second. His pants are pulled down in record time, and as he struggles to get his shoes off with his pants wrapped around his ankles, I reach my thumbs into my thong and slide them down my legs.

When I start to pull one of my shoes off, Matt's hand comes out and grabs my wrist. "Nope. The shoes stay on. Those shoes are fucking hot."

Is this guy for real? He likes me better without makeup and he loves shoes? Am I dreaming?

Before I can tell him how awesome I think he is, his hands are on my ass and he's lifting me up, pushing my back against a shelf. My legs automatically wrap around his waist.

He attacks me with his mouth while his hands are everywhere, touching me, stroking me, and making me burn with need for him. My arms move above my head to grasp onto the shelf while one of his hands slides between my legs. Two of his fingers slide through me achingly slow, circling my clit before plunging inside of me. My hips thrust forward to pull him in deeper; his tongue pushes into my mouth, matching the rhythm of his fingers moving in and out of me, and it's all I can do to hold on to the shelf when I feel my orgasm quickly approaching.

"Fuck, Paige. I love the way you feel," Matt whispers against my mouth.

My hips move faster while his fingers pump harder, his thumb circling me and driving me wild. I squeeze my thighs tighter around his hips as I tumble over the edge, my release exploding around his fingers with his name on my lips.

"Matt, Matt, oh, God!"

My orgasm is still tingling through my sex when his fingers are quickly replaced with his cock. He slides into me hard, our bodies crashing against the shelf and sending photography equipment clattering to the floor. His hips thrust against me roughly, and my body takes everything he has to give. I should feel guilty right now that I'm floating on a cloud of lust and ecstasy when my ex is most likely tied to a chair somewhere crying for his life, but I don't. Matt makes me forget everything. He makes me feel special and smart and I never want this feeling to end.

His hands clutch tightly to my hips and he helps me move my body faster and harder against him. The angle I'm in forces my clit to slide against his pubic bone with every single thrust and I already feel another orgasm within reach. This has never happened before, and I'm a little mystified at the way my body reacts to Matt; I can't get enough of him.

"Jesus, Paige. You feel so good around me," Matt mumbles, burying his face into the side of my neck, licking and sucking the sensitive skin right below my ear into his mouth.

"Don't stop, don't stop," I chant.

I feel myself coming apart around him for a second time as the shelf against my back rattles with our thrusts and a camera falls to the floor, breaking into pieces.

When he feels me coming, it pushes him over the edge. He drives himself into me two more times before holding himself still, his release spilling inside of me while he shouts my name and clutches my hips tightly against him.

Our skin is slicked with sweat and we pant against each other, trying to catch our breath. Matt moves his mouth away from my neck, kissing his way up to my lips. He kisses me softly, bringing his hand up to cup my cheek.

I want to stay in this storage closet and never leave. I know as soon as we walk out that door, real life will come calling and I'll have to deal with the mess surrounding us. At least for right now, we're alone and happy and nothing can ruin that.

"Matthew? Are you in there?"

There's a knock at the door and our lips pull apart as we stare across the room.

"Oh, my God, is that your dad?" I ask in a panic.

"You locked the door, right? Tell me you locked the door?" Matt whispers frantically.

"MATTHEW! I have to be at my doctor's appointment in thirty minutes. If I'm late, all the good magazines will be gone from the waiting room," he shouts from the other side of the door.

We hear the handle rattle and I know it's only a matter of seconds before Mr. Russo throws the door open.

With my arms and legs still clinging to Matt and his penis still inside of me, he quickly shuffles us over to the door and slams his hand against it right as it starts to open.

"Dad! You were supposed to stay in the truck!" Matt yells.

"The truck was on fire!" Mr. Russo shouts back.

"The truck was not on fire, Dad."

We hear Mr. Russo huff. "Well, it could have been."

There's silence for a few minutes and I assume Mr. Russo finally walked away.

"Do you think he knows what we were doing in here?" I ask, unwrapping my arms and legs from Matt and sliding down from his body.

"No, definitely not. He probably thinks this is the bathroom," Matt assures me.

Scrambling for our clothes, Matt helps me zip up my dress and I help him button his shirt.

"Shake a tail feather in there, you two. It doesn't take that long to put your clothes back on," Mr. Russo shouts. "Ain't nobody got time for this."

CHAPTER 18

On the way to the office after the photo shoot, I received a phone call from an unidentified man. He told me to bring the money to an abandoned building on Lincolnway West by the next afternoon or they would start cutting Andy's appendages off. I told them to start with his penis before I hung up.

The anger over what I'm doing for him makes me want to kick something, but since I'm still wearing the black Manolo Blahniks that Matt loves so much, I refrain from doing them any harm and instead pound my hand against the steering wheel.

I immediately call Dallas and let him know what's going on while I'm stopped at a red light.

"That's good. Swing by my office. I've got someone here you might want to talk to."

The dial tone sounds in my ear before I can reply and I roll my eyes. No wonder Lorelei finds him so annoying.

I leave a message on Matt's voice mail so he knows what's going on. Even though he trusts me to do my job, he still asked me to keep him updated so he wouldn't worry. Because of me he has yet another thing added to his plate to fret over. I feel bad. He should be worrying about Melanie and not about my pathetic excuse for an ex-husband.

Parking my car in front of Dallas's office fifteen minutes later, I hurry into the building and stop in my tracks when I see who is sitting in a chair in the middle of the room filing her nails.

She looks up at me and scowls.

"What is SHE doing here?" Melanie asks Dallas as he comes out of the back room and hands a cup of coffee to her.

"Dallas, what the hell is going on?"

Why would he have Melanie here? She has nothing to do with Andy. And by the looks of it, she remembers me from the night at the club when I pretended to be a drunk socialite with her and her gaggle of girlfriends.

"Melanie, this is Paige Mc—"

She cuts Dallas off mid-introduction. "I know who she is. She's the woman fucking my husband and trying to steal my boyfriend."

I'm sorry, what?

"You're separated. And what the hell would I want with the creepy old guy that you've been screwing behind Matt's back while trying to take his father's company?" I fire back.

"You skanky tramp! How dare you talk to me like that!" Melanie shouts, getting up from her chair and throwing her nail file in Dallas's direction.

"Did you seriously just call me a tramp, you home-wrecking whore?"

I don't even realize we advanced on each other until our hands are in the air, smacking at each other like two cats playing patty-cake.

"LADIES! WHAT THE FUCK?"

We ignore Dallas's shout and continue with our slapping match. One of my hands manages to make its way past hers and I grab a chunk of her hair, pulling as hard as I can.

"LET GO OF MY HAIR, YOU BITCH! THOSE EXTEN-SIONS WERE EXPENSIVE!"

"STAY AWAY FROM MATT AND HIS FATHER'S COM-
PANY, YOU SLUT!"

I pull harder on her hair and she lets out a yelp, taking a
chunk of skin out of my arm with her fingernails.

I scream in pain just as strong arms wrap around my waist
and yank me away from Melanie before I can throw any more
insults at her, or finish pulling out the chunk of weave I had my
fingers around. My arms and legs flail as Dallas moves me across
the room and far away from Melanie.

"Jesus H. Christ. Why are chicks so batshit crazy?" Dallas asks
in exasperation as he sets me down on my feet.

"Get her out of here before I kick her ass," I tell him, shooting
an angry look in Melanie's direction.

"I don't know what the fuck is going on with you two, but I
just found out this morning that the guy Andy owes money to is
this chick's boyfriend. We need her, Paige."

Whoa, what?

"I'm sorry, can you repeat that?"

Dallas raises his eyebrow at me. "Why do I feel like I just got
myself into a whole shitload of trouble by helping you out with this?"

"First, tell me something. How do you know for sure that
she's dating the guy Andy owes money to?" I question.

"A couple of calls that came through on your phone were
from a number you didn't have programmed in your contact list. I
had my guy trace the number and it was hers," Dallas explains,
pointing his thumb over his shoulder in Melanie's direction. "I
stopped by her place this morning to question her, and she sang
like a canary."

I look over at Melanie and see her pull out a compact from
her purse and check her reflection in the small, round mirror. She
straightens her hair and adds some powder to her nose before
glancing over at us.

"Can we hurry this along? I've got a yoga class in twenty minutes."

Dallas sighs and puts his back to her. "She told me she and her boyfriend got into a fight because he was talking nonstop about some hot model, and how he kidnapped her husband to try and get money that was owed to him. He was showing a picture of you in a magazine to everyone, bragging about how he was going to nail you. Melanie found your number in Andy's phone. She was going to tell you to stay away from her man, but her boyfriend snatched the phone away before she could leave a message. It seems little Miss Melanie over there is jealous of you."

"Oh please. I am NOT jealous of her. You know what? I changed my mind. I'm not going to help you," Melanie says. She turns and stalks toward the door.

Dallas runs up to her and grabs her by the arm, spinning her around. "Oh, no. I don't think so. You see, you're now an accomplice in kidnapping and extortion. You're going to help us, or you're getting a free ride straight to the women's correctional facility."

Melanie's face pales as she stares up at Dallas. "Prison? I can't go to prison. I'm too pretty for prison."

"Well, then, you're going to tell me everything you know about your boyfriend and where he's holding Andy. We'll see if we can work out a deal after that."

I clear my throat and when Dallas turns to look at me, I jerk my head to get him to come over. He sighs and walks back to me.

"Um, you don't know who Melanie's boyfriend is?"

Dallas shakes his head. "I didn't get that far with her yet. I wanted to wait until you got here to grill her more."

Biting my lip, I look up at him sheepishly. "I know who Melanie's boyfriend is. Now might be the time to call the police again."

Dallas grits his teeth in an effort not to shout at me. I have to commend him. He's holding it together fairly well considering he just had to break up a catfight.

"Who is he?" Dallas growls.

"Ever heard of Vinnie DeMarco?"

Dallas closes his eyes and shakes his head. "You have got to be fucking kidding me. The biggest crime boss this side of the Mason-Dixon Line? This is information that would have been useful, oh, say, YESTERDAY!"

With my hands on my hips, I glare at him. "How was I supposed to know Matt's case and Andy's stupid gambling problem would collide like this? You're a PI too, and last time I checked, you've been at it a lot longer than I have. Why the hell didn't YOU put two and two together, you pompous ass?"

Dallas stares at me for a few beats before a laugh bursts out of his mouth. "Well played, Paige. Well played. You might be beating Kennedy in the ball-busting department."

I lose the attitude, but keep my chin high. "So, are we going to kick a little Mob ass now or what?"

CHAPTER 19

"This is not a good idea. Can you please get your hands off her boobs?"

Matt stares angrily at Ted as he finishes up attaching a bug to the front clasp of my bra. Ted quickly puts his hands up in surrender and backs away from me while I button my shirt back up.

"I know this isn't an ideal situation, but it's our best option right now," Ted explains to Matt calmly. "We've been trying to catch Vinnie DeMarco for years. The last call that came in stated that Paige was the only one they would allow to bring in the money in exchange for Andy."

To say Matt hasn't been too thrilled about the events that unfolded in Dallas's office the other day is putting it mildly. Not only was he pissed that Melanie's Mob-boss boyfriend is the one who kidnapped Andy, he was also really mad he wasn't there to see me attempt to pull her hair out by the roots. He kissed the scratch she left on my arm and told me next time I should stomp on her foot with my Guccis. And he even knew they were Guccis. If I didn't think so before, I'm now certain he's a keeper.

Matt places his hands on either side of my face and stares directly into my eyes. "You don't have to do this. It's too dangerous."

I reach my hands up and place them over the top of his. "I'll be fine. The place will be surrounded by cops. I'm just going to walk in, hand over the money, grab Andy, and get out."

"We're not going to have her out of our sight for one minute, Matt. I promise," Ted assures him.

The door to Fool Me Once flies open and I cringe as Kennedy comes running inside, storming right over to me with a pissed-off look on her face.

I don't know what I'm more afraid of right now—walking into a den of mobsters or dealing with Kennedy's wrath.

"Sorry, Paige. I had to call her," Ted apologizes.

"What. The. Fuck?" Kennedy stutters as she stands in front of me with her hands on her hips.

"Is now a bad time to ask you if I can get a promotion?"

Right when I think Kennedy is going to punch me in the face, she wraps her arms around me and pulls me against her.

"If you wanted more work, all you had to do was ask. You didn't need to go hunt down a fucking mobster," she whispers against my hair.

"I just wanted you to see I could do something other than sit there and look pretty," I admit.

My friends know the whole story about the way Andy used to parade me around. I've never really admitted to them how deep it hurt me, though. Until now.

Kennedy lets go of me and pulls back to stare at my face. "Is that seriously what you think? Paige, I trust you. I know how smart and courageous you are. I would have never asked you to be part of this business when we met in that self-defense class if I didn't believe in you. I just wanted you to get your feet wet with easy stuff before I let you kick some real ass. I never once doubted your abilities."

It's very rare to hear Kennedy say something so heartfelt. She never wears her emotions on her sleeve. I feel a tear slide down my cheek before I can stop it. I should have trusted my friend to have faith in me.

"Oh, fuck. Don't cry. You know I don't do crying. It gives me hives. Where the hell is Lorelei?" Kennedy complains, looking around the room.

"She's in court, most likely cutting off another set of balls to store in her purse," Dallas replies sarcastically.

"One of these days, Dallas, she's going to have your balls in her purse," Kennedy tells him smugly.

"When pigs fly, dear Kennedy. When pigs fly," Dallas laughs.

"Can we please go over the details one more time so I can stop freaking out so much?" Matt asks, interrupting Kennedy and Dallas's back-and-forth over Lorelei.

"Melanie is already with Vinnie. He doesn't usually take her on jobs, but she used her powers of persuasion to convince him to take her this time," Ted explains.

"So you're saying she spread her legs. Got it," Kennedy adds. She turns to Matt and shrugs awkwardly at him. "Sorry."

"No apology necessary. Why do you think I'm divorcing her?" Matt informs Kennedy.

"Anyway," Ted continues. "Paige will go in with the money and make sure Andy is still alive. Melanie is going to start up an argument with Vinnie about his crush on Paige in an attempt to get him to admit to some of his recent activity so we can get it on tape. Otherwise, with his contacts, he'll easily find a way around doing less time. He'll be in and out of jail in no time, and then we're back to square one. This is going to be our only shot to put this guy in prison for the rest of his life and we're going to take it. As soon as we get something concrete on tape, we'll come in and arrest Vinnie and get everyone out safely."

The room is silent for a few minutes after Ted finishes his explanation.

"See? Piece of cake," I tell Matt, trying to keep the nerves out of my voice so he doesn't worry any more than he already is.

"So how do we know Melanie is actually going to do what she promised? She isn't exactly the most honest person," Kennedy asks.

"Last night, I took her on a trip to the women's correctional facility. We had a little tour. She was still crying when I dropped her off at home an hour later, mumbling about bitches with the most packs of smokes and how she doesn't want a prison tat," Ted tells her with a smile. "I may or may not have told her that as soon as she walks in the door, she'll be considered fresh meat and the words 'she's my bitch' will be tattooed on her ass."

Kennedy pats Ted on the back and looks at him with respect. "I knew there was a reason why I liked having you as a brother."

"How can we be sure that Paige isn't going to be in any danger? I mean, this is the Mob we're talking about. What if they know she's been in contact with the police and this whole thing is a setup?" Matt asks worriedly as he wraps his arms around me from behind, resting his chin on top of my head.

"There's always that risk, Matt. I'm not going to lie. But we have a couple of informants on the inside who swear there hasn't been any talk about this drop being a setup. They all just assume Paige is a ditsy model coming to bail out her ex," Ted explains.

"Dammit, now I'm jealous. Paige gets to go in there, act all stupid and giggly, and help take down one of the biggest crime rings in the state, and I have to go back and finish delivering a boring subpoena," Kennedy says.

"Wanna trade places? I can do your makeup and hair and put you in something really cute. We can practice your giggles," I tell her with a smile.

"On second thought, Paige is a much better choice for this job. Good luck." Kennedy gives me a thumbs-up and takes a seat at her desk.

"Don't be too sad. We can celebrate by getting our hair high-lighted next week. I got us a new stylist."

Kennedy scowls at me and I can't help but laugh. Laughing feels better than curling up in the fetal position in the corner, rocking back and forth in fear. It's not like I haven't been trained for this. Kennedy made Lorelei and me take a private investigator course online so we could get our PI license. But studying and taking tests online is a little easier than walking into a situation I might not be prepared for. I'm pretty sure the course never covered the topic of "Taking Down a Crime Ring without Dying." If all else fails, though, at least Kennedy made sure these last few months that my self-defense skills are top-notch.

"Paige, can you say a few things so I can test the sound level of your mic?" Ted asks as he walks over to Kennedy's desk and types a few things into the laptop he placed there earlier.

"I can take down a crime ring without dying."

Matt's shoulders slump and he hangs his head. "This really isn't making me feel better right now."

I give him a sympathetic smile and I'm overcome with the urge to tell him I love him. I don't know where that thought comes from, but it's right there, front and center and on the tip of my tongue. It's crazy, though. I mean, I just met him. Do I really love him, or am I just scared to death that I'm not going to come out of this alive?

While Kennedy, Ted, and Dallas are busy fiddling with the sound levels with the microphone app on the computer, I take the time to stare at Matt's profile. He really looks nervous and scared. Nervous and scared for me. He keeps running his hand through his hair and sighing. Even though we haven't known each other that long, I know it's a sign that he's trying to keep it together.

Matt turns his head and catches me looking at him. He comes over to me and pulls me up against him. I breathe in his fresh, clean scent and let the warmth of his body calm me.

"Promise me that you'll be careful. I need you to come back to me, Paige," he whispers in my ear.

Shame on me for thinking it was crazy to be already in love with this man.

CHAPTER 20

"It's okay, Giovanni, you can let her in."

The goon by the front door of an abandoned church steps aside when he receives his orders from across the room. He doesn't put his gun away as I walk through the doors.

The church looks like it hasn't been closed for very long; I can still smell incense from Sunday morning church services. It must have soaked into the walls. There are pews scattered throughout the huge, vaulted-ceilinged room, but some have been ripped up from the floorboards and moved around so there's more of a wide-open space. There's a large statue of the Virgin Mary staring down at me right next to the door. Even though my mother is the religious one in the family, I still say a quick prayer to her that I make it out of this alive. Hopefully she's forgiving of the fact that I am not a regular churchgoer. Or a virgin.

I swallow nervously when I see Vinnie DeMarco lounging in a pew across the room, his big, beefy arms resting on the back. I only got a quick glimpse of him the night Matt and I saw him with Melanie at Blake's Seafood Restaurant, but I've seen plenty of pictures. He reminds me of Tony Soprano: receding hairline and a belly that sticks out of his three-piece suit, proving that he has a weakness for pasta and a dislike of anything involving exercise. The butterflies in my stomach calm down when I think about all of the episodes when Tony doted on his kids and kindly gave money to the hookers he screwed. But then I start thinking about the hookers he killed and the butterflies are back in full force, trying to claw their way out of my stomach.

"Come closer. I won't bite," Vinnie tells me with a smirk.

Taking a deep breath, I make my way to him, my heels clicking on the hardwood floor, the sound echoing around the room. When I get right up in front of Vinnie, he removes his arms from the back of the pew and folds them in his lap.

"I must say, you are more stunning in person than you are in magazines, Paige McCarty."

The sound of my name on his lips gives me chills. He practically purrs and it makes me want to vomit.

"Take off your shirt."

His sudden command catches me off guard and my eyes go wide. "Excuse me?"

Vinnie gets up from the pew; his large body makes the wood creak loudly.

"Forgive me if that seemed a little forward. Sometimes I forget my manners. Would you please remove your shirt?"

I've quickly gone from nervous and scared to pissed off. Who the hell does he think he is?

"I'm not having sex with you."

Vinnie throws back his head and laughs at my statement. "As appealing as that sounds, this isn't about sex. I need to make sure you aren't wearing a wire."

Suddenly, my not-so-bright idea in the car ride over of removing the wire doesn't seem so stupid anymore. Even though Ted assured me that Vinnie probably wouldn't check me for a wire, I didn't want to take that chance. As soon as I pulled into the parking lot, I whispered a quick "I'm sorry" into the mic before ripping it out of my bra and tossing it onto the front seat.

"Giovanni, I think our guest needs a little encouragement."

Giovanni is next to me in an instant with the barrel of his gun pressing into the side of my head.

"Yep, I think that should do it," I mutter. My hands nervously reach up and begin undoing the first few buttons of my shirt.

Vinnie steps closer and raises his eyebrows. "May I?"

When I don't immediately reply, Giovanni pushes the gun harder against my temple.

Trying not to wince, I smile. "Oh, by all means."

Vinnie grabs onto the seam of my shirt and with a flick of his wrists, rips it the rest of the way open, buttons scattering across the floor as he stares lecherously at me.

I'm sure he can feel my heart beating out of my chest as he runs his sweaty palms over my skin and his fingers trace the edge of my bra.

"She's clean," Vinnie says to Giovanni.

He finally lowers the gun from my head and I can breathe again.

"What the hell are you doing?! Stop touching her!"

Melanie's screech from behind me makes me jerk in surprise. Even though I can't stand her, I'm relieved at her timing.

Vinnie sighs and drops his hands from me. "Kitten, I thought I told you to stay in the back with our friend."

Melanie stalks over to us, shooting an angry glare in my direction. I really hope this is her being a good actress, and she hasn't changed her mind about helping us. If Vinnie wasn't still standing so close to me, I'd whisper, "Don't drop the soap," just to remind her.

"I got bored back there, baby. And that guy won't stop crying. It's annoying."

That must be Andy she's talking about. At least I know he's still alive.

Melanie sidles up to Vinnie and wraps her arms around his abundant waist.

"I still have a little more business to attend to out here. Go in the back and make sure our friend is comfortable," Vinnie tells her, never taking his eyes off of me.

Melanie looks back and forth between us, and I can see her anger start to escalate.

"You just want me out of the way so you can make your move on her. You think she's prettier than me, don't you?" Melanie complains.

She moves away from Vinnie and crosses her arms in front of her in a huff. Vinnie sighs and finally turns away from me. I take that opportunity to pull my shirt back together to cover myself as best I can now that the buttons are all gone.

"Kitten, you're being silly. Go in the back like a good girl and I'll take you shopping later."

Melanie's eyes light up at the mention of shopping and now I'm convinced she's forgotten all about our agreement. She's going to screw me for a new Coach purse.

"I don't want to leave you alone with her. I don't trust her. She's going to be all over you as soon as I leave."

Ugh, as if.

"You are trying my patience, Kitten. Get your ass in the back, NOW."

Gone is the guy with the polite act, and in his place is the Mob boss. His jaw clenches as he glares at Melanie, and I watch him squeeze his hands into fists by his side.

"I don't have to do what you say! You're not the boss of me!" Melanie shouts.

Awww, shit. Not a wise move there, Melanie.

Vinnie quickly advances on her and his meaty hand is around her neck in an instant. She lets out a whimper of fear as he drags her face closer to his.

"I kept you around because you give the best head out of all the women I've had, but now that mouth is going to get you in trouble," Vinnie threatens quietly. "Giovanni, get rid of her."

Vinnie shoves Melanie away and she stumbles, falling to the ground. She tries to scramble away from Giovanni, but he quickly reaches down and yanks her up by her hair.

"NO! Don't do this! You can't kill me! If you kill me, the police will be all over your ass!" Melanie screams as Giovanni starts to drag her away.

Vinnie immediately goes from slightly mad to all-out pissed off. His lip curls up menacingly and his face turns beet red.

"What the fuck are you talking about?" Vinnie demands as Giovanni clenches Melanie's hair tighter and she lets out a yelp of pain.

"I overheard all of your conversations when you thought I was sleeping. I took notes. I made lists of all the people's names that you admitted to killing when they didn't give you the money you owed them," Melanie rambles. "If you kill me, those notes go immediately to the police, and you will be ruined!"

I can tell Vinnie doesn't believe her. His anger slowly disappears and he smiles. "You're bluffing. Giovanni, I think two bullets to the head will suffice."

Giovanni starts to drag Melanie away again, but she starts screaming.

"BRIAN CRANDALL, KEVIN BROSKY, ERIC RITCHIE, DAVE KEENER, FRANK ROBERTS!"

Giovanni halts and stares nervously at Vinnie. "What the hell, boss?"

Vinnie laughs and shakes his head at Melanie. "A few notes on a piece of paper from a whore won't stand up in a court of law. Nice try, Kitten. You have no solid proof that I had those men executed for outstanding IOUs."

If I was smart, I would turn and run out of here right now as fast as I can. Screw Andy.

"You just gave us all the proof we need. Tell him, Paige." Melanie nods her head in my direction with a confident smile.

Yep, should have run.

Vinnie whips his head around to me, and he's no longer staring at me like he wants to bang me. This look is all about murder.

Dammit, Melanie!

I should have told Matt how I felt about him when we said good-bye. I wish I had called my mother and told her that I love her even though she's a pain in my ass. Before I have time to react, Vinnie's fist shoots out and connects with my cheek. The force of the blow sends me to the ground and I land hard on my elbow. Pain shoots up my arm and my cheek throbs like it's on fire.

The sound of a gun discharging echoes through the church and I flinch from the noise.

"You touch my daughter one more time and I will blow out your kneecaps, you good-for-nothing!"

It looks like the Virgin Mary really is answering my prayers. Too bad seeing my mom again wasn't the best one for her to start with.

CHAPTER 21

Looking up from my spot on the ground, I see my mother dressed in her Sunday best, her giant revolver held steady in her hand as she points it right at Vinnie after her warning shot into the ceiling.

Oh, my God, this is not happening right now.

"MOM! What are you doing? Get the hell out of here!"

My warning falls on deaf ears as she confidently walks farther into the church, her gun held high.

"It's okay. I've got it all under control," she tells me with a calm smile.

I glance over at Giovanni. He's frantically moving his gun back and forth between me and my mother, not sure what the hell is going on.

Join the club.

"Are you insane?! You can't take out a Mob boss by yourself!"

Vinnie laughs and slides his hands in the pockets of his suit and walks toward my mother. I push myself off of the ground quickly and try to stop him.

"Please. She doesn't know any better. Leave my mother alone."

"Oh, don't worry, Paige. I think it's sweet your mother came here to try and save the day. How are you doing today, Mrs. McCarty?" Vinnie asks her with a pleasant smile.

My mother raises her eyebrow at Vinnie and lowers the gun so it's aimed between his legs. "It's MISS McCarty, you old coot."

A shot rings out and the sound is deafening in the large, empty church. Vinnie lets out an uncharacteristically high-pitched scream, clutches his thigh, and drops to the ground.

I stare in shock at Vinnie sobbing and writhing in pain on the floor, blood pouring out between his fingers.

"Oh, my God. You shot him," I whisper in awe.

My mother blows imaginary smoke from the end of the gun barrel like they did in Wild West shows. "I was aiming for his manhood, though. I'm gonna need some more practice at the shooting range."

Our attention moves away from Vinnie bleeding out on the floor to a commotion on the other side of the room. I forgot about Melanie and Giovanni. He must have lost his concentration when his boss got shot, and Melanie was able to get in a good punch to his face. His lip is bleeding and he's cursing and shouting at Melanie as she kicks him repeatedly in the shins, her hands wrapped around his arm, struggling to keep his gun aimed at the ceiling.

I don't like her, but I can't just stand here and do nothing. I'm a private investigator, dammit!

Racing over to Melanie's side, I jump on Giovanni's back like a spider monkey. I grab onto chunks of his hair with both hands and pull as hard as I can. Giovanni immediately lets go of Melanie and instead of thanking me for helping her out, she turns and runs screaming out of the church.

Giovanni's elbow connects with my ribs. The pain forces me to let go of his hair. His elbow jerks back again and hits the same spot, shoving me off of him roughly, and I fall to the ground and land right on my tailbone. The breath is knocked from my lungs, and Giovanni uses my momentary pause to catch my breath to pull his foot back and kick me right in the stomach.

I'm doubled over in pain when I hear a loud, banshee-like shout from behind him. I look up just in time to see my mother's two friends Fran and Eunice hobble up to Giovanni and start beating the shit out of him with their purses.

"YOU SCOUNDREL! HOW DARE YOU HURT PAIGE!" Eunice shouts angrily as her black leather purse connects with Giovanni's face.

"YOU'RE THE ONE WHO STOLE THE COMMU-NION HOSTS FROM SAINT MICHAEL'S!" Fran adds, hitting Giovanni in the stomach with her cane.

Getting up from the floor, I watch in awe as Giovanni cowers from their purse-and-cane assault with his hands over his head.

"STOP HITTING ME! WHAT THE HELL IS WRONG WITH YOU?!" Giovanni screams. His shouts are cut off when Eunice's purse smacks him right in the mouth.

"Don't swear at me, young man!" Fran bops him on the head with her cane.

The front doors to the church burst open then, and twenty men in uniform, with Ted leading the way, charge into the room with their guns aimed.

"GUNS DOWN! HANDS IN THE AIR!"

I automatically put my hands up so they don't shoot me by accident, but Fran and Eunice don't stop; they're too busy teaching Giovanni a lesson, connecting with every single body part of his they can reach.

The men surround the circle of angry-old-lady chaos, not quite sure where to aim their weapons. Giovanni quickly tosses his gun away and it slides across the floor.

"I surrender! I surrender! Just get these crazy bitches away from me!" he yells.

"Your mouth needs to be washed out with soap, young man!" Fran informs him as she swings her purse around and it smacks into his eye.

"Ladies! Please put the purses down!" Ted orders.

"Do I have to put my gun down too? I'm holding a criminal in place over here," my mother shouts from Vinnie's side.

"Oh, my God," Ted mutters. "Mrs. McCarty, please put your weapon on the ground."

My mother raises her eyebrow at him.

"Don't call her that. She just shot the last guy who called her 'Mrs. McCarty,'" I warn him.

My mother gives Vinnie one last dirty look before putting her gun into her purse and walking over to us. Several officers surround Vinnie, slapping cuffs on him, while one calls in an ambulance on his shoulder radio.

The cops finally get a handle on Eunice and Fran and convince them that they can take it from here. The women stop swinging their purses and take a step back, straightening their short, gray permed hair and fixing their clothes.

"It took you boys long enough to get here. I called 911 an hour ago and told them we found out who was stealing the communion hosts from Saint Michael's," my mother complains to Ted.

"Mom, what in the world would possess you to come in here with your friends in the middle of a sting?"

She stares at me like I'm the one who's lost her mind. "Paige. They stole Communion. The body of Christ. We just couldn't let something like that go, so we took matters into our own hands when the police didn't show after thirty minutes."

She shoots a dirty look in Ted's direction.

"I apologize, ma'am. We sort of had our hands full trying to take down a crime ring and didn't realize the Golden Girls were going to swoop in and save the day for us."

"Oooh, the Golden Girls. I like it. I'm Dorothy," Fran pipes up with a smile.

"You can't be Dorothy. You're not tall enough," my mom informs her indignantly.

"It's not my fault I've got curvature of the spine!" Fran argues.

One of the cops who are guarding Vinnie walks up to Ted. "Sir, the ambulance is two minutes out. We've got the bleeding stopped and Mr. DeMarco says he'll do whatever we ask as long as we keep the old lady with the gun away from him."

My mother smirks at Ted. "We might be old ladies, but we get the job done."

Ted laughs and shakes his head at her. Giovanni is cuffed and dragged out of the building, complaining the whole way about old ladies who carry bricks in their purses, and how he's going to sue the department for using excessive force. The ambulance arrives moments later and Vinnie is strapped to a gurney and wheeled outside.

My mother and her friends are taken away to go down to the police station to answer questions, and when it's finally quiet, Ted turns to me.

"Care to enlighten me on why you whispered an apology into the mic and we never heard anything that happened in here?"

Before I can inform him that taking off that mic most likely saved my life, I hear my name shouted, and I turn to see Matt running toward me. I turn just as he gets to me, scooping me up into his arms and crushing me to him.

"Jesus Christ. Thank God. Kennedy wouldn't let me anywhere near this place, and when she got a phone call that shots were fired, I thought I was going to lose my mind."

Matt pulls me away from him and runs his hands over my head, my face, my arms, and every part of me he can reach, checking for injuries.

"It's okay. I'm okay," I reassure him as his fingers lightly skim the bruise that I'm sure is now forming on my cheek from Vinnie's punch.

"Where is that asshole? I'm going to kill him," Matt says.

"Don't worry. My mother already got a head start. She shot him in the leg."

Matt glances over at Ted in surprise.

"It's true. Paige's mom and her friends snuck in the back and took care of business, angry-old-lady style: with a couple of handbags and a revolver," Ted tells him.

"Wow. Now I'm kind of regretting not bringing my dad with me. He's got a cane that he's not afraid to use," Matt adds.

"Paige, I'll give you guys a few minutes. Meet me down at the station as soon as you can."

Ted pats me on the back and then walks out of the church.

As soon as he's gone, Matt pulls me back up against him and runs the palm of his hand down the back of my head.

"I don't know what I would have done if anything happened to you today. I know we haven't known each other very long and you're probably going to think I'm saying this because of the fear of losing you, but I swear I'm not. I wanted to tell you a few days ago but I chickened out."

My heart thumps wildly in my chest. I pull back and stare up into Matt's face, bringing my hand up to cover his mouth.

"Not yet. I want to say it too, but not while I'm a complete mess with Vinnie DeMarco's blood on my pants," I tell him with a smile.

Matt brings his hand up and brushes my hair off of my cheek. "Paige McCarty, you would still be beautiful to me even if you had blood on my favorite pair of black Guccis."

Standing up on my tiptoes with a smile on my face, I wrap my arms around Matt's neck and bring his head down to mine.

"Shame on me for ever thinking you were anything like my ex."

Right before our lips touch, Matt suddenly pulls back and stares down at me. "Speaking of Andy. Where the hell is he?"

Just then, we hear a door slam open behind us. We turn to see Andy, tied to a chair, hopping and sliding his way across the floor toward us.

"Hello?! A little help here!" Andy shouts as he looks back and forth between us.

Matt tightens his hold on me and shakes his head while we stare at him struggling.

"You were supposed to help me, Paige! I've been tied to a chair fearing for my life and you're out here snuggling. I had to kick that door open all by myself and I'm pretty sure I just broke my toe. You don't even care that I almost died!" Andy complains as he continues to jump the chair closer to us, inch by inch.

Matt leans down and kisses me on the top of my head. He grabs my hand and we walk toward Andy.

"Would it be wrong for me to kick his ass when he's tied to a chair?" Matt whispers.

Andy continues to struggle, trying to get out of the bindings, and shoots us another dirty look when we finally get to him.

"Oh, my God, I can't feel my hands! You guys, I CAN'T FEEL MY HANDS! I can't live without my hands!" Andy whines.

"If you don't kick his ass, I will," I mutter to Matt as we begin untying Andy.

CHAPTER 22

All right, Paige, I think we've got everything we need. Thanks for coming down to the station. I'm sure you're ready to get home and relax," Ted tells me as he turns off the recorder in the conference room. We stand up from the table and head toward the door.

It's definitely been a long day. I'm exhausted and dirty and I just want to take a hot shower, preferably with Matt.

"Thanks for trusting me to do this today. Even if I screwed everything up," I say to Ted as he holds open the door to the interview room so I can go out in front of him.

"Paige, you didn't screw anything up," Ted reassures me as we walk down the hall. "Taking off that wire was genius. From what I've been told by Melanie in her interview, you never once lost your calm. You did good, kid."

Ted pats me on the back, and when we walk into the waiting area, Kennedy, Griffin, Lorelei, Dallas, Matt, his father, and my mother all stop talking when they see us and jump up from their seats.

"She's not going to jail, is she? I'll vouch for her," my mother says, breaking the silence.

Ted laughs and shakes his head at her. "No, Mrs.—I mean, Miss McCarty. Paige is most definitely not going to jail. She did a great job today."

My mother walks over to stand right in front of me. "I guess this job is better than you taking your clothes off all the time. So I approve."

Rolling my eyes at her, I wrap my arms around her shoulders and pull her in for a hug. "Thanks, Mom."

She pulls back after a few seconds and sighs. "Now I don't have any excuse to buy that *Maximus* magazine anymore if you aren't in it. Where am I going to get my information on *s-e-x* and relationships?"

Matt's father walks up and holds his elbow out for her to take. "How about you and I take a seat, Miss McCarty? I can tell you about the things I learned at Paige's photo shoot the other day. Did you know men wear skirts now?"

My mother links her hand through his arm. "Maybe we can exchange information, Mr. Russo. My friend Eunice told me about this new thing called roofies."

I stare in shock as the two of them go back over to the chairs against the wall to continue their discussion. Luckily, Kennedy comes up and takes my mind off of the thought of my mother slipping Mr. Russo a roofie in Jell-O salad.

"I'm going to say something right now, and after I'm finished, we're going to pretend like it never happened, got it?"

I nod at her even though I have no idea what's happening right now.

"Paige, I love you. You are an amazing friend. I even love that you force me to get my hair highlighted every six weeks. I'm sorry if you ever thought you needed to prove something to me. I have never thought of you as just a pretty face or not good enough for anything more challenging at the office. I respect you and everything you've done with your life."

This is all I ever wanted—to be taken seriously by my friends and family. The fact that it's happening all at the same time is more than a little overwhelming. The fact that it's so heartfelt and sweet coming from Kennedy is nothing short of a miracle.

"Kennedy, I . . ."

She puts her hand up in front of me. "And now begins the portion of our evening where we forget this ever happened. Good work today, Paige. You've earned that promotion. I'm going to go home now, watch football, drink beer, and do anything else un-girly that I can think of."

"You could do me. I'm about as un-girly as it gets," Griffin teases.

Kennedy looks at Griffin like she wants to rip his clothes off right in the middle of the station. She grabs his hand and I smile as the two of them walk over to a quiet corner.

Matt stands in the middle of the room with his hands in his pockets and a smile on his face. I start to walk over to him when I hear my name called. Turning around, I see Andy standing in the doorway.

"Can I talk to you?" he asks.

I know exactly what he's going to say. He's going to beg for my forgiveness and tell me he was an idiot. He might even add in a few promises that he's going to change.

Been there, done that, don't want to hear it. A few months ago, I might have given him a chance to explain and even told him that I forgive him. I've let him control the way I feel and the way I think for far too long. Lorelei was right. I'm the only one who controls my destiny, and right now, my destiny is screaming at me to man up and put an end to this bullshit once and for all.

Turning away from Matt, I stalk over to Andy and hold myself tall.

"Andy, I couldn't care less what you have to say to me. You are a pathetic excuse for a man, and I'm sorry I ever wasted my time with you. The lying, gambling, getting mixed up with the Mob and expecting me to bail you out, making me feel like I wasn't good enough for all those years—it's over. It should have been over the day I kicked your ass to the curb. Have a nice life. And if you ever even think of picking up the phone and calling me again, I will shove my Louboutins so far up your ass you'll taste leather."

Dismissing him with a turn of my body, I leave him standing in the doorway with his mouth gaping open.

Matt opens his arms and I walk right into them, burying my face into his chest.

Kennedy starts to clap from the corner of the room and I suddenly realize that everyone in here heard my entire tirade.

"That was the most beautiful thing I've ever heard," Kennedy announces.

"Is that a tear? Are you crying?" Ted asks, staring at her in astonishment.

"Shut the hell up. There's nothing more moving than watching a worthless man have his ass handed to him. I'm so proud," Kennedy says as she beams at me.

Matt hugs me closer to him and I tilt my head back to look up at him.

"So, Miss Hotshot PI, it looks like all of your dreams have come true."

I stand up on my tiptoes so we're eye level. "Not all of them. Not yet, at least."

He was seconds away from telling me that he loved me back in the abandoned church. I didn't just stop him because I wanted it to happen someplace a little more romantic. I stopped him because I wanted to make sure he really meant it when he said it. I wanted to be certain that he didn't have any lingering feelings left over for Melanie.

He looks at me in confusion and before I can elaborate, there's a commotion behind us.

"Matthew! Don't let them put me in jail!" Melanie shouts as she's taken past the waiting area with two police officers flanked on either side of her. "I forgive you for not paying enough attention to me. We can work this out!"

Her shouts are cut off as the officers lead her into the interview room and shut the door behind them.

Matt looks back down at me and when he sees the worry on my face, he smiles. "You stalked me, put your friendships on the line to catch Melanie, and saved your sorry excuse for an ex-husband. It's been a crazy month, but I wouldn't have it any other way. Melanie doesn't, nor will she ever, hold a candle to you. I'm sorry for ever thinking I couldn't trust you, Paige McCarty. There's no one else in this world I could ever rely on more."

"No, I don't need assistance with a subpoena delivery. I'm pretty sure I can handle it," Lorelei tells Dallas sarcastically on the other side of the room.

"Are you sure about that, lawyer? We wouldn't want you to accidentally cut the poor guy's balls off with that sharp attitude of yours," Dallas replies.

Lorelei huffs. "Don't you have anything better to do, like club a woman over the head and take her back to your cave?"

I roll my eyes at their typical exchange and block out their voices, content to just concentrate on the man holding me in his arms.

Sometimes you have to kiss a few frogs in life. Sometimes you have to marry a frog and then learn how to be strong again after that frog turns into an ass. But eventually, Prince Charming will finally show his face and make all those damn frogs before him worth it.

EPILOGUE

Two weeks later . . .

"Can we get everyone a refill? I'd like to do a toast," Kennedy announces.

Griffin walks around Fool Me Once Investigations and adds champagne to everyone's glasses.

I stare around the room at my friends and family. Kennedy is curled up against Griffin's side, Lorelei is shooting daggers at Dallas as he lounges against the wall, Ted is listening to my mother scold him about police response time, and Mr. Russo is standing next to Matt and me, complaining about the state of a world where nice, older women are forced to take matters into their own hands to catch a hardened criminal.

Vinnie DeMarco survived the bullet my mother lodged in his thigh and is now in jail, awaiting trial for all of his crimes. I wasn't able to get him on tape admitting his wrongdoings, but with eyewitness testimonies from Melanie and me, his fate was sealed. It also helped that he was so afraid of my mother shooting him again that he confessed to all of his sins in the ambulance ride to the hospital.

Giovanni was so traumatized after watching his boss take a bullet from an old lady, and then getting beat up by said old lady and her friends, that he took a plea bargain and gave Vinnie up. There is no way Vinnie DeMarco will be able to escape the many years of prison time that are in his future now.

My mother and her friends were hailed as heroes at Saint Michael's for their detective work in finding out who stole the Communion hosts. It turns out I was right about Father Bob looking guilty. He had a serious gambling addiction, and when he couldn't pay Vinnie the money he owed him, Vinnie sent Giovanni to the church to collect his debts in the form of enough Communion for every church service for the next five years, and every single gold chalice and church heirloom he could stuff in his bag. The Communion wasn't worth a dime to him, but it was Vinnie's way of sticking it to Father Bob. Father Bob became so paranoid that the Catholic Church would find out what he'd been doing, strip him of his clergy status, and take away his church that he began stealing money from women's purses during Altar and Rosary meetings. My mother, Fran, and Eunice caught him red-handed and made him 'fess up.

My mother apologized to Father John at Holy Cross for wrongly accusing him, and they have since asked him to join their congregation. My mother, Eunice, and Fran have also started up a community watch program called The Golden Girls: We're Armed and Dangerous. So far they have twenty-five members. I hope to God they don't all buy guns, or the police force will have to look for a new line of work.

After Melanie was questioned, she was sent off with a warning to stay as far away from the Mob as possible and not do anything stupid, or else a prison tat on her ass would be the least of her worries. The next day, she immediately signed the divorce papers for Matt and told him she didn't want his father's company after all. Vinnie had given her enough money in the year and a half they dated that she was able to save quite a nice chunk of change. She wouldn't need a job for quite a while. Little does she know, though, that that money has all been earmarked as stolen, and it will be disappearing from her bank account before she can make it to the mall.

Andy is still Andy. Nearly dying because of his gambling debt didn't change him at all. Last I heard, he decided to move to Vegas and become a professional poker player. My guess is that he'll be slinking back home with his tail between his legs very soon. Or the Vegas Mob will get hold of him and we'll never hear from him again. One can only hope.

"Everyone, please raise your glasses," Kennedy tells the room.

We all comply, and Kennedy smiles at me. "I'm going to keep this short and sweet because I think I've embarrassed myself enough lately with my girly speeches. To one of my best friends—Paige. You've annoyed the hell out of me with salon appointments and shopping trips, but you have proven to be an asset to Fool Me Once Investigations," she announces. "With your help, the South Bend Police Department was able to take down one of the largest crime rings in the city, and Fool Me Once got credit for it. I am officially promoting you to lead investigator, and you are free to handle any case that comes in."

Everyone claps, cheers, and whistles before taking a drink of champagne. I hold my glass in front of me without taking a sip while the conversations resume around me.

"Hey, why didn't you drink to that? It's awesome news and I'm so proud of you," Matt tells me.

Setting my glass down on the closest desk, I turn and cock my head at him. "I guess I'm just in shock. I mean, this is what I've always wanted—to be taken seriously."

I trail off and Matt sets his own glass down and gathers me to him. "But?"

"But there's just one thing missing. Something I never thought I would ever want again. Something I stopped believing in a long time ago," I tell him softly, bringing my hands up to cradle his face. "I love you, Matt Russo."

Matt smiles and rests his forehead against mine. "I love you, Paige. I'm so glad you thought I was a cheater."

I laugh and he presses his lips against mine. We get caught up in the kiss and don't even realize that everyone in the room has their eyes on us until we hear someone clear their throat.

"You seem like a nice young man, Matthew. But if you cheat on my daughter, there will be nowhere for you to hide," my mother threatens him.

"Don't you worry, pretty lady. I'll make sure my boy stays in line," Mr. Russo assures my mother, walking up next to her.

"Is someone going to order food? I've got to take my arthritis pills," my mother announces to the room at large.

"Are these the only chairs you've got in this place? My back is killing me," Mr. Russo adds.

Matt and I turn away from them as they begin to argue about whether food or comfortable chairs are more important to their health.

"I love you, Matt. And I even love your crazy father," I tell him with a laugh.

He tightens his hold on me. "And here I thought it wasn't possible to love you any more than I already do. Our parents are insane, but if putting up with the two of them means I get to have you for the rest of my life, then shame on me for not letting them meet each other sooner."

ACKNOWLEDGMENTS

Huge thank you to Tiffany King for talking me through my all-nighters and for saving me from rabid coyote attacks. I don't know what I'd do without your support and love. I'd probably be texting random people who would never understand my neediness like you.

Thank you to all the members of Kicking It. I love you all, and I hope someday soon we can all be in the same place at the same time.

Tara's Tramps—you guys are insane, inappropriate, and the best supporters in the world. Thank you for the "hot guy with glasses" inspiration for this book and all the improper photos you post daily to brighten my life.

Lola Stark—I'm so glad I met you! Thank you for the random inappropriate pictures when I hit my word count and for listening to me bitch and moan on a daily basis.

Thank you to Donna and Chas for organizing my chaos and making me feel less crazy. You deserve a medal just for looking at my Gmail accounts.

Janet Burns—you are a lifesaver. I would be swimming in an endless pile of receipts and banging my head against a messy office wall if it weren't for you. Thank you for making that promise to me when I left that I should call you if I needed anything. I hope you aren't regretting it now!

ABOUT THE AUTHOR

Tara Sivec is a *USA Today* best-selling author, wife, mother, chauffeur, maid, short-order cook, baby-sitter, and sarcasm expert. She lives in Ohio with her husband and two children and looks forward to the day when all three of them become adults and move out.

After working in the brokerage business for fourteen years, Tara decided to pick up a pen and write instead of shoving it in her eye out of boredom. She is the author of the Playing with Fire series and the Chocolate Lovers series. Her novel *Seduction and Snacks* won first place in the Indie Romance Convention Readers Choice Awards 2013 for Best Indie First Book.

In her spare time, Tara loves to dream about all of the baking she'll do and naps she'll take when she ever gets spare time.

For information on Tara Sivec's work, visit www.tarasivec.com.